CHUCK HOYLE

iUniverse, Inc.
New York   Bloomington

Bubble Wrap for the Mind

iUniverse books may be ordered through booksellers or by contacting:

iUniverse
1663 Liberty Drive
Bloomington, IN 47403
www.iuniverse.com
1-800-Authors (1-800-288-4677)

ISBN: 978-1-4502-5152-5 (sc)
ISBN: 978-1-4502-5154-9 (ebook)

Printed in the United States of America

iUniverse rev. date: 08/25/2010

This book is dedicated to my loving wife, Victoria Hoyle. Without her support and admiration of my work I never would have had the mental strength to persevere. If only all men were so blessed.

Table of Contents

Just a Dog

The crunching snow, ice crusted, had an effect on the German Shepard. It splayed its paws, wide as duck's feet, but was still unable to make its way through the deep crusty mass comfortably. The German Shepard, old and lazy, looked around the white countryside and then back to the owner, as if for some sort of direction to extricate itself from the frosty mass. She urinated, and then sniffed around for a place to defecate. Upon completion, she pranced her way back to the owner. Panting and galloping through the deep snow back to where the owner was standing, tail wagging like a well propped fan, she came up and started to lick the old gnarled hand offered to her.

"You did your business," said the old man. "You're a good dog."

The old man stretched his legs and patted the large dog on the head. He turned to the house and hobbled on his one good leg. The ice was treacherous for even those with two good legs, but for him, it was a nightmare. The dog followed, still observant of the surroundings of ice, snow and a squirrel in a tree, but wanted to keep up with her master's progress. The dog sniffed to the left and then to the right, ate some snow then went into the house.

A fire in the small house kept the domicile warm. When it was very cold the old man would have the dog sleep on his lap. The electricity had been out for several days and there were no lights and the kerosene lamp was running low. The old man turned up the lamp, took up a magazine from the small brown coffee table, and invited the dog to come up on his lap.

"Shazam," he said uttering his dog's name, "Don't worry, life gets better than this." He rubbed the side of Shazam's head and continued, "I've seen worse days." The dog came up on the couch and rubbed its head in the old man's lap. "Oh Shazam, you think you have lived a long life," the old man intoned, "but the things I have seen could put a troll in a hole and a young man darting for shelter." He patted the side of the dog's head and went on. "I've seen young girls cry, old women die, and young men slap the side of their hip with their chest puffed out just before being blown to pieces by a mortar shell." He stroked the long ears of the dog, each ear rotating like some sort of radar. "I'm not a hero Shazam, I was just lucky. Heroes are lucky too. Courage is overrated. Every hero I have known is now in the ground."

The dog looked up into the face of the old man with its resonate dark brown eyes, rotating its head this way and that with its soft, meticulously cleaned fur brushing against the old man's leg. The dog had two black rims over the top of her eyes, resembling eyebrows, and like a human's eyebrows, they worked up and down, imitating human's expression; one down in suspicion, one up with intrigue, both up in surprise, or both down in a pouting expression.

"Carnage," said the old man as the dog slipped its tongue in and out intermittently, in small abbreviated bursts, as if trying to taste the air around it, "that's what they used to call me back in the service. I would cause carnage. I didn't even know what the word meant back then." He leaned over and kissed the dog on the nose. "I hope you never have to learn what carnage is."

Stroking the ears of Shazam and then patting the black and cream colored side of her the old man went on, talking to his dog like the friend she had become, "I've seen things no-one should see." He looked to the ceiling, while still stroking his dog, "The worst thing is that there is a total lack of understanding. People don't want to know what I've seen, and I guess I don't really blame them for not wanting to know. Why should horror be a side-show? I guess most people have had wretched experiences in life; Why should they listen to what's in my own closet of horror?" He grabbed his dog in a bear hug with his callused hands and added, "Little girl, I wonder sometimes if you have a closet of horror, but I hope you don't."

Shazam responded by licking the man's face. The old man pointed his face to the ceiling one more time, letting the dog lick his chin rather than other parts of his countenance. "Kisses, kisses, you're always wanting to give kisses." He pushed the dog back to his lap. He then laughed. "I used to get kisses from women, not just dogs." The old man gave a sigh and the grin disappeared from his face. "I've told you before about your mother. She used to want to give kisses. Then there was nothing but bitterness and hatred. So it goes, little girl." He stroked his dog's face. "Love drifts to a point of not caring and then to hatred, I just wish there were somewhere to go back." He hugged the dog one more time.

Just then a knock came at the door of the small apartment. Shazam started barking and jumped off her master's lap. She went to the door and continued barking, loudly, in rapid fire, barreling off a contentious fire of snarls between the snapping. The old man pushed himself to his feet and went to the door. He pulled Shazam back by the black, leather collar. "Shush little girl," he said quietly, and then opened the door.

On the other side of the door was a young man familiar to the old man. He was wearing a blue suit with a bright red tie. He was thin and had the close cropped hair of the military man he had been. He was holding a large briefcase and inexplicably lowered his head to inspect his shiny black shoes before offering his hand to the old man. Shazam snarled at the offered hand, and the young dark haired man recoiled.

"Shazam," the old man implored to his dog, rubbing the side of its face. "He's a friend. He's a friend." The old man looked at the young man in the entryway. "She won't bite Karl. You know that."

The young man edged in against the ecru colored walls of the entryway, positioning himself as far as he could get from the growling dog. He looked into the house, noticed some garbage bags on the floor, the moth eaten green sweater on the old man then shook his head back and forth. "Walter," said the young man, adjusting his tie on a fine suit, "may I come in? And could you please put Shazam somewhere else?"

Walter, the old man, stroked the side of the aged German Shepard. He looked at the young man's wonderful, dark blue suit, bright red tie, and was taken aback by the contrast to the bright white shirt underneath. "You look great Karl," the old man wheezed out, still holding onto Shazam. He reached down to pat the head of his beloved dog then tilted his head up to Karl. He made a fist and stuck it toward Karl. "That's what you have to do. Dogs understand that. Don't stick your fingers out. Just make your hand like this and let them sniff."

The young man swallowed hard then looked again around the front room. There were newspapers on the coffee table along with some dirty dishes and a water stained ceiling. He clinched up his right fist and cautiously leaned it out toward the growling dog. He had been afraid of dogs since grammar school and felt like wetting himself. He squint his eyes shut and held his breath until the growling ceased and he felt a large tongue lapping against his knuckles. When he opened his eyes, the large Shepard was indeed licking his hand and he almost buckled at the knees. "Oh shit Walter," he gasped out, with an enormous exhale. "Would you please take that thing somewhere else?"

Walter stroked his dog over the brown head one more time. The human like eyebrows of the canine went up and down, first to the left, then to the right, showing a human like understanding. "Hell Karl" Walter said with a quizzical expression, "she's all I got. I don't have any family. I hardly have any friends." He leaned down and scratched under the dog's chin and continued." What I know, she knows. What she knows I know. It's not like anything you tell me will be spread around the neighborhood by Shazam." He noticed Walter's paling countenance, and re-orientated his thoughts. "There's no reason to be scared. Shazam hasn't ever bit anyone. She just likes making noise. Hell, Karl, she's better than a burglar alarm." The young military officer kept his grim expression. "Okay," Walter said and then instructed his dog while giving another pat on the head. "Go lay down." The dog dutifully went to one corner of the room and lay down with a low and lingering grunt.

Karl's pulse and respiration slowed as the large dog retreated. He looked at the dog in the corner, which was looking at him and imagined some sort of cognition in its face. "I'm going to bite your balls off," she said to him in the resonance of his mind. Karl then pulled a piece of paper out of his jacket pocket. "Here Walter," he said, "this is the reason you need to call the VA. It's pretty self explanatory." As he handed the piece of paper to Walter, Shazam lunged from her spot in the corner and intercepted the piece of paper with a growl.

"Bad girl," Walter said while pointing a finger at his dog. "He's a good man. Now give me the paper. Give it. Now, damn it, give it." He held out his hand and Shazam relinquished the paper. "Now go back to your corner." Shazam hesitated, inexplicably sat down, wagged her

4

tail, and finally replied to the request by walking slowly and sullenly toward the corner her master was motioning to.

The young military officer was back to panting and wanting to urinate. He had both hands splayed against the wall. He pulled loose one hand, slowly, as if it had been glued there, and rubbed it across his short greasy head of hair. "Please sir," he said, "read the paper. That is if there is anything left of it." He took the one hand free from the glue on the wall and pointed a shaking finger at the wrinkled mass. "There," he said, "sir, the information on that paper is very important to your status with the VA." He gave a furtive glance to Shazam in her corner, which was starting to growl again. "It's very important that you reply right away."

Walter read the letter out loud, after pulling a pair of cheap reading glasses from his pocket. He adjusted the glasses and stretched the piece of paper back and forth until it was again readable. "Walter Reed," he started as he leaned back from the document, "It is our duty to inform you that your benefits will be henceforth canceled due to your lack of communication with this office. While we acknowledge your valiant service, your decorations and service to our country, you, as a veteran, should know duty has a lifetime of service. If you wish to contact me you may do so…"

Walter stopped, gave Karl an angry stare and then crumbled up the paper. "I should have let Shazam eat this," he said. "I have two bronze stars from tours in Korea." He shook a fist in the air. "I spent hell crapping in pits in the Pusan perimeter, shooting with what little ammunition we had left at a relentless foe. I dug trenches, ate garbage, drug the dead and wounded away from battle lines and made midnight forays into enemy lines to guide artillery." His voice amplified as he threw the paper to the ground. "You're telling me you can take away what I've earned just because I didn't answer some screwball?"

Shazam noted the anger and angst in her master's voice and came over to him. She started rubbing her face on his side, leaving a residue of hair wherever she touched. She pranced around manically in a circle a few times while Walter kept his fists clinched. She came back to her master, rubbed the side of her face one more time, and then let out a wide mouthed, nervous yawn. Shazam then sat down on her haunches and looked up and into the face of Walter for direction. She leaned out to lick Walter's clinched fist and her eyebrows did another dance.

Walter unclenched his fist and patted the side of her head and said, "Baby, I'm not mad at you. Go back to your spot. I just have to get some business done." He gave Shazam a small push on her shoulder and added, "Go on sweetheart. I'll be done in a moment."

The attention was then turned to Karl. "How can they do this to me?" he said with a more muted tone and tears welling in his eyes. "I've been a hero that no-one has recognized, in a war no-one cares about, and now I'm being thrown away by the government that drafted me, sent me there, and gave me medals for bravery. Can you explain this to me?"

"I have to explain," said Karl, adjusting the lapels of his fancy jacket, then sheepishly going on, lowering his head a bit. "I mean, don't kill the messenger. I mean I don't make these decisions." He held up both hands, palm forward, close to his face. "Sir, I understand your consternation and have utter respect for what you have accomplished on the field of battle. Your accomplishments are the major reason why I have been sent here. People at the VA thought you were worthy of an extra attempt at rehabilitation."

"Rehabilitation," said Walter, while rubbing his forehead with one hand, thumb and index finger on each temple, his voice now a whisper. "What do they mean by rehabilitation? I have earned a full retirement from the army. What is there to be rehabilitated from that? Two bronze stars, a purple heart, just what makes that an issue of rehabilitation?" Shazam got up from her corner and brushed against her master's leg. And then she looked up into the face of her master. "What does this mean?" said Walter, rubbing the side of the dog's face and having a tear exit his eye.

"You were," started Karl, again stepping back from Shazam, "supposed to fill out forms for your benefits. They are fairly easy to do. I have copies of them here in my briefcase if you want them." He fiddled around in his briefcase and pulled out a thick file to offer to Walter. "Here, we have gotten these together for you. I'm required to tell you to fill these out in one week or your benefits will be terminated."

Walter took the file with his left hand while rubbing Shazam's head with his right. Shazam looked up at his folder then stood up to sniff at it. She sniffed at it until her black nose left a small smear on the outside of the manila folder. She then gave a small whine and sat between her master and Karl. "Who sent you here?" asked Walter.

"Uh, I'm not supposed to say. But it was an old colleague of yours. It was Major Johnson. Please don't tell him I told you. Please sir."

"Johnson huh?" Walter took the folder and tossed it to a small couch near Shazam's corner. "If you were allowed to tell me, then I would tell you that Johnson could stuff this stuff. But I won't require you to do that. I don't want to kill the messenger. But I will be down there tomorrow to have a talk. I won't tell him you told me. But that idiot needs to be talked to. Now, please leave my house." Shazam, sensing a change in her master's mood, started to growl at the visitor, and Walter reached down to hold her by the collar.

Karl backed to the door holding his briefcase across his chest and said, "I'm sorry sir. I again commend you on your service." He then opened the door and closed it quickly behind him.

Walking over to the couch, Walter looked blithely at the folder and let out a giggle. He picked up the remote control for his television and took a seat. "Come here Shazam," he said, "come up and keep your dad company." Shazam, haltingly, stretched out and leaned up onto her master's lap. "That's a good girl," Walter said giving a kiss to the long nose. "I know you didn't like that man, but it wasn't his fault." He stroked the side of Shazam and continued. "People just do what they are told to do. It isn't like you and me, where we can do what we want. So don't be mad at him." The old man leaned over and kissed the dog on the nose one more time.

"Shazam," he said, "do you remember the time we walked on the beach?" The dog's tail began to wag. "Do you remember when you were afraid of the deep snow?" Shazam climbed all the way up on the couch and placed her two front paws on her master's lap. "Do you remember your mother?" He leaned over and patted the dog's haunches. "She was very nice to you. She used to give you treats and rub your hips when you were limping." He slapped her backside one more time and laughed. "Do you remember when we put you in the back of the truck to take you to the lake and you had a diarrhea fit and rolled around in it? That really disturbed your mother. I didn't care much though." Walter leaned down to kiss his dog's long nose again. "I wish your mother was here to see how well behaved you are. I wish she was here to see how you have become such a good girl. But mommy had other plans." He bent and gave his beloved dog a hug.

Shazam roused off the couch and shook her head, rattling the tags on her collar back and forth making a ging-a-ling noise. She opened her mouth wide in another yawn then flopped to the floor. Almost in the same motion, she began stroking a paw across her face, then started clawing at the carpet. She twitched a bit then closed her eyes. Her breathing seemed a bit labored and Walter leaned to the floor to stroke her side. Shazam let out a low groan in her sudden sleep and stopped twitching. The gentle undulations of her breathing gave Walter comfort.

Walter noticed the slight red color on Shazam's neck. When she was very clean, it was apparent. She had just been to the groomers and all of Shazam's colors seem to come out vibrant and compelling. The groomers always commented on how beautiful Shazam was, which filled the old man with pride; a pride he often mused on. Was he proud for the dog, or proud of a possession he had? The groomers always gave Shazam a treat when they finished. Shazam would sniff and let it drop. When she was nervous, she would never eat.

The old man stretched and bent his aching back to pet his dog. "I'm proud of you. That's the answer.

"Do you remember when I used to take you to the fountain at the college? You used to prance around in the shallow water with all abandon. I used to worry about you licking the chlorinated water. But, hell, I've swallowed enough chlorinated water in my time from swimming. I don't suppose it really harms you. But you started thinking all bodies of water were only knee high. When me and your mommy took you to the lake you jumped off the pier thinking you were going to splash around and sank clear under the water only to come up whimpering and whining. Mommy wanted me to jump into the water and do something. But I knew you could swim. That's why they call it the dog paddle. I knew you could do it. You swam right back to the shore." He pulled on the dog's collar and added, "Come up here baby, keep me warm, you're my only friend."

Shazam came back up on the couch and lay on her master's lap. "I guess I'm going to have to go down to the VA and talk to a knot head tomorrow. What do you think of that?" Shazam let out a low groan. "Yeah, that's pretty much how I feel." He stroked the lovely Shepard and said, "Those are the same sort of groans I do when you vomit on the carpet." Walter then wheezed out a long laugh.

"You know what little girl? I'll bet you miss your mother. I know that I do. She was always good to you. I remember how she used to put ribbons around your neck at Christmas time and the way you seemed to be happy at some sort of decoration like the Christmas tree. I was happy with decoration. When they pinned the medals on me, those were my decorations. I felt as happy as a Christmas tree." He hugged his dog one more time.

"Time gone by and mind gone away," Walter said with a smile, continuing to pat his pet. "There wasn't much I couldn't do when I was young. But I'm old now and things just take more time, energy, and thought than they used to. It's too much trouble to keep up with technology. Heck, most of the time I don't really want to try."

Shazam rolled over onto her back; all four paws bent and recoiled into her legs then gave a mild whine. Walter started scratching the white underside of his dog.

She slept on the bed with Walter that night, on the white comforter put there to diminish the sight of all the dog hair deposited there. Walter had to wash it once a week and it was getting threadbare from the use. He felt his companion twitch from time to time but Walter went into an uneasy sleep. His dreams were alive and vibrant. Just as soon as he rolled over, away from Shazam, he went into a world of horror not available to most mortals. The ruined relationships, the calculated response to all sorts of calculated attacks aimed at him from people he used to call friends entered his REM sleep. He twitched and found himself awake and panting. He looked to Shazam, who was sleeping peacefully, and gave her a gentle pat.

"How are you doing little girl?" Walter said, rubbing the dog's side. "Life goes on, even if it isn't a good life." Walter sat up in bed. "Life goes on little girl, even if things seem bad. That's the magic of life." Then he noted the time on his bedside clock. It was time to get up, wash, and head down to the VA. He had an appointment and the old veteran, who had seen flags draped across coffins, twenty one gun salutes, and the carnage of battle got up to wash himself in the shower, and went to his appointment. As he was leaving, he patted Shazam on the head. "I'll be back in a little bit my sweet little baby. Sleep as long as you like."

After the meeting, Walter was quite angry. The VA had demanded the litany of paperwork and Walter had refused. He told them it was their responsibility to give him what he deserved. The young, well dressed handsome man had infuriated Walter with his smugness. It was such a nice office, Walter thought, to have such horrible consequence. It wasn't definitive yet, but the wheels were turning to abrogate all he had earned. It was galling for Walter having to talk to some sort of desk jockey about his benefits and he let his emotions show.

Entering the house was a relief. While walking up the well manicured lawn, he let his mind drift to all sorts of wretched memories. There were the times in the senseless battle of war, when he was sending men into zones of danger where his thoughts were unknown to him. At these times, he didn't allow himself to think. But, for some reason, away from the horror of battle, all he could do was think. Flashes of his wife came into his mind. The sound of artillery echoed in his mind. There was a time when these things hadn't bothered him. But this was a case beyond the pale. After all he had been through in his life, after so much he had done for his country, he was absolutely distraught wondering how they could get away with doing this to him. Yet this was home. He walked in the door with a military pose and let out a long laugh.

"Screw those ingrates," he said, adjusting his thin leather belt, "they wouldn't know pumpkins from raisins. Why should I care? I'll find something to do."

He walked into the bedroom and Shazam was still on the bed. He sat near the head of the bed and started venting his frustration. "Little girl," he started, "these guys are trying to steal all our money." Walter licked his lips, stared off and away and continued. "I've done more than most humans could do in five lifetimes in service to this country. I shouldn't complain. A lot of other men gave more."

Walter giggled one more time. "That little twerp at the VA, I told him to shove his head up his butt so that he could tell me where all this crap was coming from."

He looked to his beloved dog and patted her side with a wide smile. Shazam didn't flinch, as per usual, and Walter patted again. Then he gave Shazam a shake. "Wake up little girl. Your daddy is home."

All at once, Walter saw that there was no breath, and that Shazam felt unnaturally cold. "Get up baby," yelled Walter. "Oh please, just get up."

Pulling Off the Job

Philip sat on the couch polishing his gun with a rag with the appropriate oil. He liked the way the barrel shone after he was done. It glistened. It had a good feel on the handle. He spun it around like the old west movies and put it into the holster he had on the chest, similar to those used by detectives. He pulled it back out, spun it one more time and stuck it back into the holster as if he was practicing for some sort of competition. He leaned over to the dresser, took out some tissue, and wiped his hands free of the oil.

He looked around the room, an adequate motel room with sparse appointments, and started thinking about the day's plan. His partner, Marty, would be coming soon. He needed to be ready. The gun was oiled. He had drawn a diagram of the store. Marty had given him several things to do and he believed he had nearly done them all. He hadn't, however, followed up with getting the phone number of the store. Numbers bothered Philip. He would explain this to Marty when he came along. Philip was sure Marty would understand. It was early in the morning and Philip reasoned this was to his advantage for not having done something he was supposed to have done.

He took out the gun one more time, inspected it, smiled and put it back in the holster. He then took several practice attempts; seeing how fast he could yank the gun out of the holster and stuff it back in. He did this over and over, sometimes spinning the gun around before putting it back. The glistening barrel gave Philip a sort of excitement, a sense of power. The smell of the oil, the possibility of shooting it for the first time, the intrigue of what was to be done all filled him with excitement.

Taking out the gun as fast as he could one more time, he spun it like a cowboy. Simultaneously, a knock came at the door. Philip, startled at the knocking, squeezed the gun and it went off into the ceiling. The roar of the gun left him with ears ringing, and more dazed than usual. He stared at the end of the barrel, pointing it in between his eyes wanting to know what had just happened. The smell was new to him and he pondered how it might have smelled on a battle field with so many guns firing. He grinned into the small caliber hole as if he could return to the momentary pleasure the gun had just brought him.

While lost in his enamor with the pistol, hand still on the trigger, barrel still pointed between his eyes, another rapping came at the door. Philip twitched, nearly shooting himself in the face and he stood up. He shoved the gun underneath the mattress and started running around the room thinking about what he would say as an excuse for blowing a hole in the ceiling. He could always just play stupid. That was easy and easy to prove. He had done it many times before and everyone always believed he was stupid. He just didn't want to go to jail again. He had just gotten out. One night stands in the county joint were a common occurrence to people like Philip: vagrancy, public drunkenness and the like. When he had quickly exhausted his options for figuring a way out of this mess, all reason lost him, and he ran into the bathroom and locked the door.

Marty rapped on the door again. "Open the door Philip," he hissed. "Open the damn door you idiot. Did you shoot yourself or what?"

Marty tried the door and it was open but had the door chain attached. Marty pressed his face into the crack and whispered, "Hey, Philip, are you there man? Man, I'm gonna have to break the door if you don't answer me."

Philip could vaguely make out his friend's voice. He unlocked the bathroom door and peeked out. Stepping slowly out of the bathroom, he realized, suddenly he was in his underwear. For some reason, this problem took precedence before answering the door. He went running around the room looking for his trousers.

"Open the damn door," whispered Marty, face stuffed into the crack between the chain and door jamb.

"Wait a minute," yelled Philip, trying to buy time, embarrassed at his near nakedness. He then went to the door and jammed it shut. "Just a minute," he shouted.

On the other end of the slamming door was Marty's nose. He let out a squawk and began flapping his arms like a bird and produced noises akin to one. "Open the fucking door," he screamed in a nasal tone, nose thoroughly wedged, "Open the fucking door, you idiot,"

The pants were found by Philip in his battered suitcase. Normally he would have put away all of his clothes by now into the dresser. He pondered why he hadn't put his clothes away. The idea of being untidy was foreign to him. There were people, in his mind, who didn't handle the important things in life before handling the essentials. He went on wondering about this until the screams of his friend entered his brain. But he retrieved the gun from under the mattress. He wanted to show his friend his new persona; one of "Macho Gun Guy."

"Open the fucking door," screamed Marty in agony.

Philip unhooked the chain and popped the door open, surprised at how hard he had to yank it. Marty stumbled backward into the parking lot, falling and knocking his head onto the bumper of a car. "You damn idiot," said Marty holding his face with both hands. "What the, what the, what the hell are you trying to do to me?'

"I was cleaning my gun, man," said Philip while opening his flimsy, ragged dress jacket to show Marty the gun with holster. He grinned large, and felt on the cusp of something wonderful. The threadbare jacket tore at the shoulder when he reached over to pull the gun out. "Cool, huh?"

"Put that thing away," hissed out Marty, motioning with one hand while trying to stand, holding his nose with the other. "Do you want everyone to know we got guns? Put that thing away."

Marty got to his feet, going back to holding his face with both hands; blood was dribbling down the sleeves of his fine white shirt from his nose. He was a dapper dresser and this irritated him greatly. He walked past Philip and into the bathroom. He tried to control the bleeding by shoving two large wads of toilet paper into either nostril, being as delicate as possible; then tried to wash the blood from the cuffs of his shirt. With toilet paper emanating from both nasal holes, blood staining them, he came back out to the bedroom.

In the interim, Philip had decided Marty was correct about the need to conceal his gun and decided to hide the gun again. He neglected to take off the holster; he didn't give it a thought. Thought wasn't much of his concern. He put the gun back between the bedsprings and mattress at the foot of the bed then pulled it back out again. He knew there was a safety, the switch preventing inadvertent firing, but was confused as to its position. He had switched it back and forth, got disgusted, and then just put it under the mattress.

Marty came out of the bathroom, two nostrils with hanging toilet paper, and said, "How stupid are you?" His nose was discernibly swollen. "What the hell? Give you a gun? I might as well give a monkey a machine gun. Hell, you can't even operate a damn door."

"I'm sorry about your nose," said Philip, "but I didn't have any pants on."

"Screw your pants you idiot. I don't care if you had to come outside butt naked with your hair on fire to get me loose. What the hell is wrong with you?" The two trails of paper continued to absorb the crimson liquid.

"I've got an idea," said Philip. "We've got to go and be fast. Let's go and get…"

"Shut up stupid," yelled Marty, voice still reflecting his swollen and bruised nose. "When I want stupid opinions or stupid things said. Then I will call the Mr. Stupid hotline and ask for you. Mr. Stupid is all I'll have to say. Everyone will know who you are. I won't even have to say your name!"

"You shouldn't call me stupid," said Philip, face curling into a pout, "that's not nice."

"My nose almost got cut off you idiot. What do you think about that?"

"Idiot is a nicer word than stupid," Philip said, adjusting his worn and torn jacket, "I thank you." Then he plopped onto the lone chair of the room.

Marty paced back and forth for a few moments, heels of his black shoes spinning on the cheap carpet. He felt like kicking something but didn't. He went back into the bathroom and saw the two huge plugs emanating from his swelling nose and the now greenish rings around the bottom of his eyes. He came out of the bathroom and saw Philip; he wanted to smack him in the face. Instead, he plopped down onto the foot of the bed.

The gunshot was muffled by the mattress, but audible and had blown out the window. Apparently the safety was off. The motion of Marty's butt on the bed had discharged the weapon. The two men stared at each other for a moment. Then Marty looked down between his legs checking for injury, feeling at his crotch and buttocks. He then picked up the end of the mattress and found the gun.

"You idiot," yelled Marty, "You idiot. You idiot. What the hell are you thinking?"

He shook the gun in Philip's face. "You think these things are toys?"

"Well," Philip said, "someone has to be a rookie once. I mean, there was a time…"

"Shut up! Shut up stupid."

Just then there was a knock on the door. Marty and Philip stood frozen. The sound of the highway traffic, which ran in front of the motel, became horribly apparent. Marty had grabbed Philip by the collar just before the rapping on the door and the two began to exchange glances between themselves and the door. The knock went again and louder. Then one more time, which could only be described as a banging.

Marty walked to the door and started to open it forgetting to hide the gun. He pushed the door shut when it was half way open tossing the gun to Philip. Philip started playing cowboy with it again, spinning it on his finger. Marty ran over and wrestled it out of his hand. "Put that thing somewhere where it can't be found you moron. It ain't no toy." He then started back to the door when he saw Philip lift up the end of the mattress. "And not under the mattress stupid, you want me to blow my ass off."

"You don't gotta get sore," said Philip, scratching the side of his head with the well oiled barrel. "I'm not Mormon anyway. I hate those guys."

The hard banging on the door came again.

"Put that thing somewhere," Marty hissed. "I don't care if you shove it up your ass. Just get it out of sight."

Philip gave another expression of pouting. "I tried to put it under the mattress but you wouldn't let me. Why don't you just tell me where to put the damn thing? And I'm not putting it up my ass."

The banging came one more time, this time with a voice. "Open the door, damn it, or I'm going to use my key and just come in. Or I'm going to call the cops."

15

Marty opened the door partially with a small grin. The face of the grizzled, old, unshaven proprietor of the motel pushed close to the opening. All the proprietor had on was a sweat stained, white polo shirt and some sweat pants. He noted the two wads of toilet paper trailing out Marty's nose. "Someone just blew a hole in my window," he snarled. "And someone is gonna pay for it, or I'm calling the cops." He reached in and pulled the door shut.

Marty turned to his partner in crime and said, "What the hell is wrong with you? What the hell do you got to do other than sit down and be quiet?" He started shaking his hands on either side of his head. "But, but, but, you have got to do stupid things like this."

"I didn't sit on the gun. I guess who's stupid now?"

"You stupid jackass!" yelled Marty, starting to pace the room again. "I didn't know the gun was there." Then, flapping his arms, "Never mind, never mind, I just have to think for a while." He started to flop onto the end of the bed when he looked to his comrade. "Is that thing still under here?"

"What thing?" said Philip?

"Damn it," screeched Marty, "I've known donkey's assholes with more sense than you. The gun, the gun, I'm talking about where you put the gun. You know the thing that blew a hole in the ceiling and the window out? You think I want to blow out another window?"

"It wasn't my fault," Philip said. "You sat on the bed all by yourself."

It wasn't until check out time that they had settled the bill for the window and set out for their mission of the day. Check out time was noon, they barely made it, and the sun was already high and hot in the sky. The compact car they were driving was old, dilapidated, and quite conspicuous amongst the commuters, rattling with a trail of smoke along the thoroughfare. Philip was driving and Marty started rapping on his arm.

"Hey, hey, there's a great taco stand up here. Pull over," Marty said. "It's one of those vans. It's always here. But they got great food and I'm starved."

"I'm not eating at any 'Roach-Coach,'" said Philip piously.

"Pull over stupid," screamed Marty, "we'll stop somewhere else that fits your palette later. OK?"

Philip stood steady on the steering wheel for a moment, cocked his head to one side then asked, "What's a palette?"

"Never mind," snapped Marty, "just pull in here. I want some tacos."

The old van had been parked in the hot sun all day. It was necessary to move it out of the public parking lot at night, by law, but returned in the early morning to catch the migrant crowd headed for the fields, lawns, or whatever they were doing that day. There was no health inspection. There was no place to wash hands or use a restroom. It was a large van, equipped with a stove and a pot of over-used grease. The refrigeration unit rarely worked for the food stored there and so the proprietor let it go on its own, not having the funds to get the refrigerator working properly. Most of his customers didn't complain, because most of them came before nine in the morning.

"Pull over," Marty ordered. "I want some food."

"Alright," said Philip, swerving the raggedy car into the gravel lot, "you get what you want. But I'm not eating that crap."

"Suit yourself, but this stuff is great."

Marty got out and walked up to the little window on the side of the van. The sun was unrelenting and stung his eyes. He scratched the side of his face and noticed that the owner was starting to finish and clean up from a days work. Noticing the urgency involved with getting an order, he rapped on the little window. The owner waved his hand, looking side-long at the potential customer, "Closed," is all he said.

Marty stared at the window as if he could blow it open with his eyes and smacked his hand flat on the window. "Hey, you, I want some tacos," he said. "And I want them damn spicy. Hot. You know muy calliente. Got it? Do you got it? I want four of them and damn pronto."

The proprietor looked around the van, inspected some of the contents and relented. It had been a slow day. This rude white man would get his tacos, but the quality would be suspect. He knew the food he had leftover was probably spoiled, but if this guy was so desperate, he would get what he wanted. The van owner went to the window, sweat hanging from his chin, a chin having not been shaved or bathed in several days. The sounds of crickets could be heard chirping in the background. A slight breeze could be felt as he opened the sliding window, easing the humid furnace which was inside. He had already sent his help home for the day and would do this alone. He had been a short order cook for years so this would be easy, and he needed the money. The menu signs were down, so he would charge this dumb white guy double.

"Si senior," the proprietor said in a false accent he used on white people – he had been born and raised in Irvine California. "Four tacos will be coming up, extra hot. I mean muy caliente."

"That's better," said Marty rapping on the small counter.

The owner of the tattered van grabbed all the things destined for the dumpster and proceeds to make four tacos. The meat was overly fragrant, the cabbage wilted beyond recognition and he had to pick flies out of the salsa. He had a half can of extra hot jalapenos sitting in the suspect refrigerator, which were hot even to him, and he laced them onto the tacos, making them very hot as had been commanded. He rolled them up in some paper, carefully, and brought them to the window.

"Here you are sir, uh, senior." He had forgotten his accent for a moment. "I hope you like them. Uh, fifteen dollars."

"Fifteen dollars? For four damn tacos? Are you out of your mind?"

Marty looked around the landscape, then at the tacos in the box which had been handed him, then back to the grinning proprietor. Marty was hungry and he didn't want to fight over tacos so he said, reaching into his pocket to produce a twenty, "Here, keep the change."

He started munching on the tacos in the car without a word to Philip. He was peeved with the way he had to command Philip to the place where he wanted to eat. He finished off the first taco and started in on the second when the spiciness of the jalapenos began frying the inside of his mouth. They were hot, as he had demanded, but they were as hot as the dark side of the moon is cold. Marty tried not to say anything, and just put his second taco back into the little cardboard box. Sweat began to bead on his brow. He looked to Philip. Philip looked back.

"So, how are the tacos?" Philip said. "Is it everything you remember?"

"Yeah," gasped out Marty, wanting to pant like a dog, "just, you know, like things I can't forget." He held motionless for a while, and then threw the remaining tacos out of the window screaming, with both hands coming to his mouth as if he could pull the spice out, "Get me some damn water. I'm burning up. Don't we have anything to drink? Why don't we have anything to drink?" Tears rolled down his face as he spoke.

"There isn't anything to drink," Philip said calmly. "We are in a desert. Why do you think that there would be water in a desert? And you are the one calling me stupid."

"OK, I won't call you stupid anymore, just get water," said Marty hanging his head out of the car like a hound, tongue flapping in the breeze. "I need something to keep my head from catching on fire."

Just about that time, Marty started to feel another sensation. The taco and a half he had eaten began running a track meet through everything lower than his esophagus. He pulled his head back into the car then stuck it back out. Nothing seemed to work. He couldn't decide whether to vomit or crap his pants. He pinched up really hard and looked to Philip. Philip looked serene with his docile face. Marty wanted to slap him. Marty's colon tensed up again, causing him to twitch. As if contractions in birth, the diarrhea attacking him now was coming and going and wouldn't be alleviated until the expulsion of the thing causing the havoc. It felt as if some sort of beast was trying to claw its way out his sphincter.

But the spasms had its pauses. And in one of those pauses Marty asked Philip, "So, you got the address of the store we're going to knock over?"

Philip looked puzzled and then said, "We're going to kick over what?"

Another spasm went through Marty's body and he actually rose up his hips and squint his eyes. "You idiot," he yelled. "That's what we are doing. That's why you got the gun. We're going to rob a store. Got it? Got it?"

"Well, at least you didn't call me stupid," replied Philip. "But what store and where?"

Marty's jaw drooped a little. He let out a little gasp and ran a hand across his scalp. He could feel his colon puckering one more time. "The store we're planning to rob you moron." He jabbed a finger into Philip's face. "The store we've been planning to shake down for six months. Do you even have the slightest bit of a clue?"

"I told you," said Philip judiciously, "that I'm not a Mormon."

"That's moron you stupid ass. M-O-R-O-N. Not M-O-R-M-O-N. Not the dudes who bang on your door, it's the dudes that bang their head into walls wanting bananas. Do you get the difference yet? You are a moron, not a Mormon. Where the hell is this store?"

"Well," Philip started out, "I believe it is…"

"Stop the car," Marty bleated out.

"Why?"

"I have to take a dump, and I mean now. Oh great God, I mean now."

"Hmm, I told you not to eat at that stand where the conditions…"

"Shut the hell up," said Marty, "and stop the damn car."

"There's a gas station ahead, I'm sure they have a toilet and we need gas anyway," said Philip, feeling good at finally having some sort of control over the current situation.

"Hurry, damn it," yelled Marty.

Marty ran into the station holding the cheeks of his buttocks pinched shut with both hands hoping this could help not having anything eject. An eerie scowl was on his face. It was a rather large gas station, with the usual large array of sundries, which made the bathroom hard to find. Marty went to the back, where the bathrooms usually were, then came rushing back to the counter where he pushed in front of several customers.

"Where's the toilet, man? Where's the toilet?" he asked, doing a little dance.

The clerk, an older gentleman, with large red lips, belly drooping over his tucked in white shirt, was in no way in a hurry to help a patron who had pushed their way to the front of the line. He looked Marty up and down, hair loose and all askew, and sized him up to be some sort of loser, which he was, but the desperation in Marty was lost on the clerk. He merely saw some sort of loser, dancing while holding his butt cheeks.

"Come on man, where's the toilet?" said Marty while starting to do a little jump with the dance while holding his butt. "I mean really. I need the toilet."

The clerk rolled his eyes and said, "The toilets are only for customers. Are you a customer?"

"My friend, the guy I'm traveling with, is filling up outside right now. Where's your goddamned toilet?"

"Don't you swear," Said the portly clerk, pointing a finger speaking very slowly, "and don't you use our Lord's name in vain. If you want to use my toilet, you will ask me politely, and kindly. Otherwise, forget it."

"Okay, okay," Marty said quickly, "please sir, may I use your toilet? I really need it."

"Now that's better," drawled the clerk. "Now you just get back into line and we'll get to you when it's your turn."

Marty did a little jog around the store, half the time bent over from the stress of not messing his pants. In his maniacal dance, he realized he had a little bit of cash in his pocket and came up with a plan spawned by desperation. He grabbed a few items off the shelf and slung them up on the counter, pushing his way in front of other patrons again. "Here," he said, "now I'm a customer. Now show me where the toilet is."

The clerk rolled his eyes again, shaking his head so that his chubby cheeks shook. The clerk couldn't hold his disgust. He took the items, one by one, as he rung them up in the cash register. There were only three items, but it took him at least a minute and a half to ring them up. He searched around for a bag to put them in, as if he had done this for the first time, then put them in a flimsy plastic bag and handed them to Marty who was stressing from the strain.

"Now you may use the toilet," said the clerk.

"Where is it? Where is it?" said Marty continuing the dance, pinching at his butt cheeks with both hands.

The clerk, in no hurry and irritated at the young man's demeanor, paused for a second then said, "It's over behind the milk."

"Okay, okay," said Marty as he started toward the milk refrigerator.

"Wait a minute," yelled the clerk behind him, "somebody's got the key. That means it's in use. You'll have to wait until they get out."

Marty ran to the back of the store, behind the milk refrigerator, and tried the door. Initially it seemed locked, but he shook feverishly at the handle and the door opened. When he thought he was on the cusp of success he realized it could be failure. Inside the bathroom, there was only one stall. He could see a woman's stiletto heels coming out from underneath the door. He heard her say, "Who's there? Who's there?"

By the time the second 'who's there' came out, Marty had knocked the lid off of the bathroom garbage can, dropped his pants, and swung himself up on the square opening. Without any effort, immediately, he evacuated his colon and let out an audible, "Ahh." He could finally relax, halting the effort of puckering. It had exhausted him. He had propped himself up by his hands on either side of the garbage can and let loose when his colon had let loose. He suddenly slid into the garbage can, knees wedged almost to his chin and arms clumsily stuck straight up. He wormed this way this way and that but was as stuck as a bug in a spider's web.

The young, good looking woman with the stiletto heels flushed the toilet and came out of the stall. She saw Marty in the garbage and acted aloof. She washed her hands and then dried them with the blower on the wall. She looked at him one more time before exiting; it was a look of complete disgust.

Marty flapped one arm, which was propped into the air by the wedging garbage can. "A little help please," he said with a smile as she passed by, only to have her continue out and slam the door. "A little help here, hey, a little help here."

As Marty wiggled, trying to get free, it only caused him to sink lower. Like a man in quicksand, Marty was slowly sinking into oblivion, knees in the face and arms protruding useless.

Just when Marty was going to forget any sort of decorum and start screaming for help, he heard a voice. "Is this occupied?" It was Philip.

"Get in here stupid. I need help," Marty said from his sinking condition. By now his voice had become strained and muffled.

"Who is that?" said Philip.

"It's me you stupid moron. Come in and help me."

Philip pondered what had been said for a few moments. He then realized it was Marty who was on the other side and snapped a few words through the grey door, "Don't call me stupid."

"I'm talking to you, you dumb mother fucker, come in and help me!" He sank a little lower. Had he not been very flexible, he probably would have strained several muscles by now.

"I'm not coming in until you apologize for calling me stupid."

Marty struggled as hard as he could, face turning red, grunting and groaning, but only succeeded in sinking an inch lower into the feces lined container. "Okay, Okay," he yelled to the door. "I'm sorry. I'm so damn sorry that my mother is sorry too."

"What are you sorry for?" said Philip to the scratched grey door.

The struggle ensued again, with futile results. After reaching a point of absolute desperation Marty said, "Okay, I'm sorry I called you stupid. I'll never call you stupid again. Okay?"

"Then I will come in and help you," Philip said, then rattled the handle. "It's locked. I think I need a key."

"You don't need no damn key. Just wiggle the thing. It will open."

"I'm going to go and get a key," Philip said as he spun around to go to the counter.

"Hey, hey, hey," screamed Marty, "get in here. Get in here." By now his heels were sticking straight up in line with his arms, pants to the ankles, butt drooping into his own excrement along with used paper towels.

Philip got in line with the other patrons then saw an article in a tabloid displayed next to the register. He got out of line and went over to read it. "Alien Babies Found in Desert," it said. Philip wondered, if while he and Marty were in the desert, if they would find any alien babies. Hmm, Philip went on with his cogitation: if there were alien babies then where were the alien mothers and fathers? His mind raced with the idea of alien women. He wondered if they were hot or not. From the picture on the tabloid of the babies, he deciphered that if they looked anything like their parents, they were not hot. But maybe they just liked to have lots of sex and that's why they leave their babies all around.

As he put down the paper, he could hear a muffled screaming coming out of the restroom. He suddenly re-realized his purpose. He walked to the front of the line and asked the clerk, "I need the key to your restroom... please."

With the key, Philip popped open the door. He saw his companion in the garbage bucket and said, "What are you doing in there?"

It took a bit of effort to extricate Marty. He groaned and moaned from the effort, not the least of which was straightening out his contorted torso when he finally got out. Pants around his ankles, he stood and stretched, groaning and moaning loudly. He squinted his eyes shut and twisted this way and that. When he opened his eyes, he saw a troop of people at the register watching the scene: the door was still open.

"Close the door dumb ass," hissed Marty.

Philip looked around at the back of his companion and said, "Ew, you stink. And you better find a place to take a shower. You've got taco crap all over you."

"Close the damn door," Marty hissed again and then tried to bend over to pull up his pants. His back was so stiff he staggered, and with pants around his knees he stumbled forward and into the main part of the store, launching headfirst into a stack of cereal boxes. Philip, dutifully, closed the door from the inside and made sure it was locked.

Philip finally found the directions to the store. They drove there with the windows open to keep the odor down. They pulled into the wide parking lot, seeing many cars much finer than any they had ever ridden in. After they parked, a woman pushing a shopping cart walked by and started sniffing in the air like a blood hound on the ground. She gave a glance to the car and kept walking. Marty slouched a bit, and rolled up his window.

"Okay," Marty said, "it's time to rock and roll. I'll get the ski masks." He reached behind the seat and pulled out two, black knit, wool ski masks. He tossed one to Philip and said, "Put it on."

Marty pulled on the wool ski mask, fussing with the attitude and alignment of the garment. He pulled down the passenger side visor, which had a mirror, and checked his look. He had seen crooks in movies wear these things. They also had them on videos he had seen. Marty wanted to look as cool as all those guys in the movies and videos.

"Hey," said Philip, "I can't see. What the hell good is this?"

Marty turned to his would be companion in crime. "You got it on backwards, you dumb ass." And truly, Philip had the sock-like head garment directly opposite of the way it should have been. When viewed from behind, the two eye holes and mouth opening gave the appearance of some sort of poorly constructed jack-o-lantern.

"Turn that thing around," yelled Marty. "Here." He said yanking the ski mask off of Philip's head. "Put it on like this." He jammed the mask onto Philip's head making sure it was oriented correctly. "Okay," he went on, "you can see now, right?"

Philip adjusted the wool mask and said, "Yeah, I think it works better this way."

"Okay," Marty said adjusting his belt as if readying for a fight, "now give me the gun."

After a small pause, Philip said, "Gun?"

"Yeah, dumb ass, give me the gun." He looked over to Philip. "I said, give me the gun. Now!"

"It's hot in these masks," Philip responded, then squeezed his hand up underneath it to scratch his cheek. "And the damn thing itches."

"We'll only have to wear them for a minute if you would only give me the gun. It's hot, damn it, let's get this over with."

"You told me to hide it," said Philip.

With eyes bulging right through the mask, Marty screamed out, "Now find it. I want you to find the gun now."

Philip sat listless for a second then said, "I hid it in the motel room. I forgot…"

Marty slapped both hands to the side of his head and screeched, "What? You stupid ass, dumb shit, retard, piece of monkey dung, what were you thinking? We needed that. How the hell are we going to do the job without a piece?"

"A piece of what?"

"The gun, you stupid, moron, idiot fool."

"Well, I hid that in the…"

"Shut up," screamed Marty. "Would you just shut up?"

Just then, there was a rapping on the passenger side window; both men, ski masks fully in place in the ninety degree heat, sitting in the closed compartment of the car and stench beginning to foment. Marty looked to the window. It was a security guard for the store. He was old and hefty. His face was ruddy and had a sneer. He was rapping with a Billy club and did so one more time.

Marty rolled down the window. "Can I help you?" he said; black ski mask drawn over his face.

The security guard initially recoiled from the smell, but then leaned back toward the window, "Just what the hell y'all doin' sitting here with these masks on?" he said. "It seems a bit hot to be wearing them things; shouldn't you take 'em off? Or should I call the cops?"

The two in the car exchanged glances, "I was cold," said Philip, "and, and I have a skin condition. You really don't want to see it. I mean, it is ugly. My aunt Gertrude had the same thing, but you would never know it. She wore lots of makeup. But I don't like to wear makeup, so I wear this." He looked to Marty and continued his monologue; a grin was viewable from the slit for the mouth in his mask, "And my friend here wears one to make me feel comfortable with myself. You know he even…"

"Shut up!" screamed Marty and pulled off his ski mask in disgust. "We were just leaving officer; just plain leaving."

Philip took off his mask, with sweat matting his hair, and gave Marty a strange look. "You know Marty, he really isn't an officer. He's just a…"

"Shut up you stupid bastard!"

"You promised not to call me stupid," said Philip calmly and quietly, resuming his pout, "I want to go home."

"Yeah," said Marty, giving a small wave to the security guard, "we're going home."

Interpretation of the Clouds

Jabbing at the air with one index finger, holding a briefcase and puckering his lips, Ernie let out a groan knowing what was coming. The two big brown doors of the conference room loomed large as he walked down the hallway. He adjusted his red tie and then made sure his fly was up on his blue trousers from his last stay in the bathroom. There were many papers in his file and as he pulled them from his case and went through them some of the papers fell to the floor. As he stooped and collected them, the large brown doors opened. He looked up and a stoic looking man, which he correctly guessed as being a secret service agent, gave him a small sneer. Who else would be wearing sunglasses and an earpiece in such a dark place?

Though the diminutive man scooping up the papers had been through security in order to get into the building, the secret service agent was required to pat him down prior to seeing the three congressmen. The small pudgy man called himself Ernie though his name was Ernest; a name meaning devotion and honesty. He had been through the pat down drill before, but always felt uncomfortable when it came to feeling around his groin region. When the pat down was done, Ernie realized he had been holding his breath during the pat down and then wheezed out a puff of air when it was done. After an inspection of the briefcase, the stiff, suited, sunglass wearing man motioned with an index finger, without a word, for Ernie to enter the room.

In the room, looking like a miniature of a Congressional hearing room, there were three congressmen. The one to the left of the oversized desk, a grey haired man from Nebraska, looked bored, leaning one hand on his cheek and eyes half shut. The man in the center, a bare bald man with a black fringe from Iowa, gave a small grin of recognition to Ernie. On the right was a chubby red faced man Ernie did not recognize. He was from Alaska and had the blubber which would be the envy of any whale in the Arctic around his drooping jowls and black hair greased back in a pompadour as if he had exploited some whale oil to do it. Ernie took his seat and at first looked at the steely gazes, then busied himself with getting his notes out of his briefcase.

"I thank you for your time, Congressmen." Ernie started hesitantly, interjecting pauses between most words, hands beginning to sweat. "My report is complete. You have my sincere apology that it took so long to complete."

"For the record," the bald man in the center said lackadaisically, "state your full name and the purpose of this meeting." He finished off his request with a peculiarly bland expression.

"My full name is Ernest Falcone Falconi. I am here to address events regarding the data retrieved from the Valkyrie probe." He licked his lips and noticed the lack of cognition from the congressmen. "It's the probe sent by NASA to Venus."

"I'm aware of the probe," interjected the congressman from Nebraska. "I have an engineering degree from the University of Chicago. You don't have to lecture anyone on what went where to what. Are you listening?"

The blubbery man on the right interjected, "Why was the name Valkyrie chosen for this particular project?"

Ernie cleared his throat, thumbed through his notes then replied, "Valkyrie is a Norse word meaning 'chooser of the slain.' It is a metaphor for those who die in battle." Ernie paused for a second, thinking of all the thousands of hours he had spent on the project. "We knew that a probe to Venus," he went on, "would be doomed in several hours and thought the name Valkyrie would be appropriate, being as how we knew it would soon die." Ernie rubbed his sweating hands across his head. "Die as in service to our purpose."

The blubber man started his interrogation. "Young man, you obviously are an accomplished carrier of information and there are no reasons for this body to find you incompetent." He paused with a wide, chubby cheeked smile then continued. "However, we do have information that you might be having some problems with your management. Would you like to address this issue?"

Ernie scratched the side of his head, wondering who, at his place of work was undermining his report, then said, "Some constituents in my organization do have questions about the conclusions we have come to. But I should add that I'm not the only one who, with help, added to, and came to the conclusions I will present to you today." The suspicion and thought of people he worked with sending out rumors to congressmen or their staffers stung him like a bee. "My management is free to its opinion of me," he added, "but I am free to follow the truth of the data."

Blubber man continued, sticking out his hand, "We, speaking for the American taxpayer, have spent a lot of money on this project." He paused a bit and sat up straighter. "Just what the hell has this Valkyrie accomplished?"

Scratching the side of his head again, Ernie shuffled his notes one more time. "I need to tell you some, well, interesting information. I believe this will fortify the rationale for spending so much money on this project."

"Nothing," said the bald man in the center sternly, "I could imagine would tell us how this money was spent and how this project was worthwhile. But me and my colleagues here on the board will try and keep an open mind."

The white haired congressman from Nebraska roused himself and stared at Ernie. "What kind of name is Ernest Falcone Falconi?"

Ernie sat back in his large leather chair and then said quietly, with a questioning knitted brow, "Sir, uh, Mr. Congressman, that's my name."

The Alaskan congressman snapped out, "He's asking you a question." He adjusted his fancy suit and went on. "You will show this panel the respect it deserves. I've been in public service for thirty years. It's probably longer than you have been alive." He then shook a meaty index finger toward the young NASA employee. "You will show respect."

Ernie looked to one side, away from the waggling finger then adjusted his notes one more time. "I meant no disrespect in answering your question sir."

"Disrespect," roared the white haired man from Nebraska, "hell, that wasn't even a word a couple of years ago. You could have said 'lack of respect' or something like 'I didn't give you the proper respect' but you said 'disrespect.'" Then in a derisive tone, "Why didn't you go ahead and say what the kids are saying these days, something like 'dissing?' He then let out a hearty laugh. He leaned to his fellow congressman in the center and added, "These kids, these days, what can you do?

The congressman from Iowa held up one hand to stop the ridicule and had noticed a bit of alcohol on the breath of his colleague. "My distinguished colleague from Nebraska," he said addressing the colleague, "we are here for information about the Valkyrie probe. We are trying to find out why and where the probe ended and what information, scientific and otherwise this report has to offer. Why we spent taxpayer dollars on it, and why we haven't heard any news about it."

"Ah hell," the Nebraskan said, "quit being so formal. This isn't a hearing it is only an informational do-dad. If you want congressional protocol to be followed then have a full hearing."

The bald, Iowa congressman rolled his eyes. Then the Alaskan voiced his opinion. "We should get to the mark. I mean, fan the flames and get the fire started. We have a lot of things to do today. Let's spark this thing up and burn out this little fire. I have a lunch date with people and I don't give a dang about Valkyrie but I'm supposed to care. But we will never get anywhere if you two keep talking."

"Your comments are well noted," said the slick headed man in the center, "now let's get down to business." He stared intently at Ernie and continued. "Please, let's make this as quick as possible."

"Distinguished gentlemen," started out Ernie. "I…"

"Distinguished gentlemen," roared out the white haired congressman. "What the hell is that? Just talk to us boy. Talk. We don't need a butt licking, we want information and we want it now. We all got important business to do."

The slick headed man in the center who had thick black eyebrows raised his hand once again to signify silence. "Please," he said, "let the young man talk." He then directed his attention toward Ernest, "what information have you brought here that is so important to interrupt our daily duties?"

Ernie fumbled through his notes one more time. "Uh," he started, "there are some extraordinary findings from the data from Valkyrie. As

I'm sure you well know Valkyrie wasn't just a probe, it also had mobile capabilities upon landing. We programmed into Valkyrie some special features."

"What," said the man from Iowa, "did you teach it how to put on make-up?"

Looking to the center congressman, Ernie continued to mess with his papers. The silence in the room struck him all of a sudden. Outside, on the street, the noise was cacophonous with garbage trucks and semi-truck and trailers. He was only behind a couple of doors and there was no noise at all. The lack of noise caused his ears to ring and made him less focused. The most disconcerting thing, however, was being under the glare of three important men who he had to tell some disturbing facts to.

"Valkyrie," started Ernie, clearing his throat, holding a fist to his face, "was programmed to have survival instincts. You see, we wanted it to last as long as possible. So, if you are aware of the Venutian climate and atmosphere, it is quite harsh for any mechanical device to operate for long. The surface temperature averages 467 degrees Celsius. That's hot enough to melt most metals. I guess we wanted to get more bang for our buck." Finishing, he let out a little nervous giggle.

"Boy," said the red faced congressman from Alaska, "get on with what you are going to tell us. All three of us have things to do, things that matter. If I wasn't part of the committee, I wouldn't be here, but listening to this drivel is making me want to leave. Is there anything of substance you have to offer to us?"

"Sir," Ernie said, beginning to stammer, "I, uh, I, uh, have some important information. How... wow... however, it might be a bitter puh, puh, pill to swallow. I, uh, mean, it's kind of unbelievable." He finished off his sentence by shaking his head back and forth like a wet dog trying to extricate itself from water.

The bald headed man in the center sighed, shook his head, rubbed his hand across the desert scalp, and bent his head. "Son," he started, "would you please get to your point. Believe it or not, we have other things to do."

Ernie fiddled with his papers one more time, but this time quickly. "Uh, sir, Mr. Congressman, uh, distinguished congressmen we have spent a lot of time evaluating the data retrieved from Valkyrie. It isn't necessarily definitive. However, this is our best conclusion."

"Get on with it boy," the white haired man from Iowa intoned. "When you finish I have to take a pee then go get a cup of coffee; important issues of the day, you know." He finished by putting his head back on the palm of his left hand, picking up a pen and doodling on a piece of paper.

"Sir, uh, Mr. Congressmen," Ernie said, getting more annoyed with the grilling, "I have information which might change the way we look at the world. Uh, I mean the way we look at our place in the universe."

The congressman from Nebraska erupted, "Get on with it."

Becoming terser, Ernie responded, "Sir, I have an engineering degree from MIT, and I don't enjoy being berated when I have information which could drop the scales from your eyes and am trying to convey it."

"Don't get smart with me," the Nebraska congressman said.

The bald pate man in the center raised his hand one more time, signifying some sort of sign for the want of a verbal cease fire between the two. The two combatants acquiesced and the congressman from Iowa added, "Mr. Falconi, would you please get to the point."

Ernie cleared his throat, and shuffled his papers once again. "Valkyrie, as I've told you, was programmed for self preservation in the harsh Venutian environs. This is part of how we, the group at NASA, wanted to have the maximum amount of data for the money spent." After the words 'money spent' went out, Ernie gave the congressman from Nebraska a nasty look.

"Get on with it," snapped out the Nebraskan.

"I have," Ernie said, "evidence from our data, and telemetry that shows some strange things." He noticed the unrest in the three members of the inquiry and continued quickly. "As I've told you, Valkyrie had survival software programmed into it." Ernie started kneading his hands together. "Apparently, with all our best interpretation of the data, Valkyrie found a tunnel, uh, I mean cave, to find shelter from the heat. The probe was sending a fantastic amount of information up to this point. When she went blank, all of us assumed she had failed."

"Why do you refer to this NASA event as 'she'?" the Blubbery congressman from Alaska asked.

After a moment of thought, Ernie said, "its name's origins are of the beautiful maidens attendant upon Odin who bring the souls of slain warriors chosen by Odin or Tyr to Valhalla and there wait upon them. Therefore, I decided, not a decision of the agency, but I decided to refer to the Venutian rover as a she." He gauged his response on the panel and added, while shifting his eyes back and forth from each of the three well dressed congressmen, "How would you like to have me refer to Valkyrie? It is hard, after years of work for me to refer to Valkyrie as an 'it'."

"Young man," the red faced man from Alaska said, "Just calm down and wrap this thing up. Do you know what I mean?"

"Yes sir," said Ernie, blinking his eyes and with a big sigh. "I need to tell you what happened and what we have been doing. Valkyrie, he, uh, it went to this cave to seek some shelter from the heat. While she, I mean he, I mean it entered the cave, there was no communication. However, from time to time, apparently the rover would come out of the cave to send data. We were quite surprised Valkyrie lasted so long."

"Yes, and I'm surprised this is lasting so long," said the Nebraskan. "Could you please boil this down to a few bullet points?"

"Sir," Ernie went on, still twisting his fingers back and forth in front of him, "this isn't easy to say. But one of the last transmissions from Valkyrie indicated that she, I mean it, had found a friend. Something in the cave, described by Valkyrie as her, uh, its friend relayed a lot of information about Venus. The information was unintelligible for a while, which is why we took so long to make the report. It seemed like some sort of code, at first, but we found patterns and pieced together messages. It appears that our rover was going in and out of the cave, balancing the need of preservation with the need of its primary directive of communication."

The chubby faced Alaskan, jaw agape, eyes wide open, said, "What the hell do you mean 'a friend'?"

"That's, um," Ernie started, "what Valkyrie called it. We don't know exactly what it was, but it seemed to be programmed to tell a story. We're fairly sure it was some kind of computer. Perhaps some sort of time capsule. It seemed to be a time capsule from a dying civilization. How Valkyrie found it is considered totally serendipitous by most, however, I have my suspicions that Valkyrie was detected by this device and was called into the cave."

The white haired man from Nebraska stood and said, "I got to go use the toilet," and then exited the room using a door behind the large desk. The other two men had looks of amazement, especially the man from Iowa.

"Are you sure," the Iowan started, "that there was some sort of transmission between Valkyrie and some sort of alien being? Or did the harsh conditions of the planet Venus cause malfunctions in the software and bring about some sort of gibberish?"

Ernie took a deep breath. "Sir," he started, "I can assure you that the information we received from the last transmission was something not capable of Valkyrie's data base. To be honest, we thought at first it was just gibberish. But we have some very capable people imbued in the art of encryption. One of whom you might be familiar with is Dr. Frooman, the gentleman who helped decipher the Soviet codes in the early eighties. He noticed, along with others, certain patterns in the seemingly random data. It took months and thousands of man hours, but we came up with a method to decipher the data."

The blubbery Alaskan shivered his head back and forth setting his jowls into a gelatinous, vibrating mode which didn't slow quickly. "You mean to tell me Mr. Falconi," he said, offering out another beefy hand, "That there is alien life on the hellish climate of Venus?"

"No sir," Ernie said, "maybe I'm not being clear."

The door behind the desk had just opened while Ernie stated his last sentence and the white haired Nebraskan, looking a bit more frazzled, stumbled into the well appointed office and plopped back onto his chair. "Then get to the point, damn it," he barked out. "What the hell is more being clear than being clear, if you don't know the difference between being clear and not being clear, then you don't belong here? You need something between your ears." A grin came over his face and he turned to his fellow congressmen, "that was a rhyme, right off the cuff," he said chortling. "I can do that all day."

The bald Iowan leaned over to his colleague and whispered in his ear. "Gerard, you're getting drunk, which is fine with me. But you need to shut up and listen." He then turned back to the young NASA official and said, "Please continue."

Gerard, the Nebraska congressman, waved his arms in the air and said, "Poursuivre petit. We won't bite." He then gave the man from Iowa a knowing nudge with his elbow, with one eyebrow raised and a grin. He whispered back into the chairman's ear, "This boy don't got a snowball's chance in hell. Do he?" The Iowan responded with a look of indignation, realized the inebriation factor, and turned back to the NASA employee.

"Please go on," the bald chairman said. "We are finding this quite intriguing." He looked to his right, noticed his slumping Nebraskan colleague, who was drifting in and out of conciseness and added, "Well, at least most of us are." Whereby his colleague dropped his head onto the desk and let out a low moan.

"Mr. Chairman," Ernie started, again reshuffling his paperwork, "we have gathered information from her, I mean the probe, I mean the rover Valkyrie which is quite incredible."

"You seem to have a bit of affection toward the probe. Do you think this might have influenced some of your conclusions?" the bald man asked.

"Perhaps, if I had been working alone," responded Ernie, pulling his tie this way and that, still being nervous at having to give the report. "However, I've been working with a team, and this is just not my conclusion alone."

The blubbery Alaskan chimed in, "Then what did this thing, entity, or time capsule as you worded it, have to say?"

Swallowing hard, Ernie looked into the faces of the two cogent congressmen, noted the one passed out on the desk, and started. "It appears, from the data translation, there once used to be a sophisticated society on Venus. From the data we found, there were songs, dialogue, some of which was not decipherable. Then there was a warning, a very clear warning of doom. From the machine, computer or whatever it was which communicated with Valkyrie we found out that it was put into this cave nearly fifty thousand years ago." The young man cleared his throat, paused and continued repeating more slowly, "Fifty thousand years." He gave a little cough and finished with, "Valkyrie asked this thing, whatever it was, how it had survived and it said it told Valkyrie it had a geothermic cooling system. How this communication went on, we don't know. Valkyrie wasn't designed to communicate with something else. Our theory is that this thing, whatever it was, picked up on our telemetry, frequency, and made a connection. Why it didn't, having deciphered Valkyrie's ability to communicate, translate things more completely is a mystery.

"Apparently the society on Venus, whoever they were, created this instrument to warn visitors of certain aspects of what had been their behavior. It seems they had become aware of their demise and this instrument, whatever it was, was designed to give a warning to those who might one day visit. This warning, after moving in and out of the cave to send transmissions, came from the last transmission from Valkyrie. Apparently she succumbed to the heat. She was programmed to send and receive messages. We couldn't send her messages when she was in the cave. So, she kept coming out to receive them, and send data." Ernie's eyes began tearing and he retrieved some tissue from his jacket pocket, wiped his nose and dabbed at his eyes. "With all due respect, sirs, this was a heroic adventure and I'm sorry I'm getting emotional over an inanimate object. But I spent so much time, energy, and emotional toil on her. I can't imagine the courage it took to come out into that thick cloudy mist of sulfuric acid and heat just to send us data. It had a friend in a place where she could be safe." He finished by blowing his nose.

"Your reaction is duly noted," said the congressman from Iowa. He paused, and then added, "You should really compose yourself." Then rubbing his bald scalp once again, the chairman asked, "And what was the behavior these, well, people were trying to warn us of? Well, I guess anyone, not just us." He leaned forward much more intrigued and tried to ignore his snoring colleague. The blubbery Alaskan also leaned forward.

"The best translation we can get from the data," Ernie said, "and we are still working on it. But we believe the warning was a single word, which was 'overindulgence'. It was a reference to doing too much, for too long." Ernie lowered his head. "Terraforming is the word people sometimes use. Apparently these aliens, Venutians if you will, transformed their planet into a place uninhabitable through their actions." Ernie raised his head and looked at the two functioning members of congress and added, "It's a warning in my opinion humanity, on earth, should take seriously."

Is and Was

(The setting is a world renowned news organization television studio. There is a flash on the screen saying, "Breaking news." A very thin woman named Leslie, in a nice suit, comes on the screen with a serious expression on her face)

Leslie: This just in, professor Hartford of Eastern Illinois University has just published a report predicting that, "We are who we once were." The professor says this theory was established over a period of twenty years of careful observation of the student population of at least one University. For more on this shocking theory, we now turn to our legal advisor, Harry Bestial. Harry, what about that notion that we are who we once were? Or, perhaps better phrased, we once were who we have become. Harry?

Harry: Well, I've known professor Hartford for a lot of years and he has always been prone to hyperbole. However, given his lifelong passion of deciphering the human condition, one cannot categorically throw out his conclusions.

Leslie: Are you saying that there is some credence to the notion that we, as humans, more specifically, American humans, can surmise, quoting directly now, "We are who we once were."

Harry: What I'm saying is that the works of Dr. Hartford should not be discounted. I think the notion of being now what one used to be is an idea which requires more thought.

Leslie: And what are the legal ramifications of this controversial assertion?

Harry: It's hard to say. One never knows how the court, especially the high court, will rule on the premise that "once having been will regulate what one will be," but I don't think it will cause any major bombshells, especially in an election year.

Leslie: Thank you Harry. For more on the subject we have invited a dissenting opinion from Dr. Henry Householder of the Forbes Institute. The Forbes Institute is a Washington based think tank based on the study of Political Awareness, Being and Spoiled Milk. Dr. Householder, what do you make of Dr. Hartford's assertion that we are who we once were?

Dr. Householder: Absurd. How could we possibly be who we were when we're different from who we have been? I mean, rational people from all over the world realize the difference in the English language between "was" and "are." It doesn't take much explanation. If he were trying to delineate the distinction between, "what we could have been," and, "what we should be now," then I might hold out a scintilla of hope for his muddled conclusions. But this is really a thin charade of ivory tower rhetoric so distanced from reality I can't support it.

Leslie: Can you expand on what you mean by, "what we could have been," and "what we should be now?"

Dr. Householder: I feel it is self-explanatory. What we could have been is a notion of what should have been; a sort of intellectual 20-20 hindsight. What could have been is a conditional sense of the past. Not what was, necessarily, but a venture into the possibility of what had been. Ergo, what we should be is a conglomeration of ideas into the possibility of having the feelings we have not met the mark of how our inkling of being fits with what is.

Leslie: Thank you Dr. Householder for those insightful remarks. We turn now to Mark Westman in the field who has been monitoring the day's events. Mark? What is the latest on Mr. Hartford's controversial theory?

Mark: I'll tell you, it has been complete pandemonium in front of Dr. Hartford's residence ever since the publishing of his thesis. You can see the news vans parked on his lawn behind me and across the street a small group of student protesters have gathered.

Leslie: Are the protesters saying what they want?

Mark: Yes Leslie, they seem concerned that there is no "is" in Dr. Hartford's theory. The protesters are also disturbed by the lack of a singular pronoun; specifically the absence of the pronoun "I."

Leslie: Hasn't there also been developments in the University itself?

Mark: That *is* correct, and I use that conjugation of the verb "to be" carefully now. Sources close to the Doctor say he has come close to relenting the 'What We Were is Now Who We Are' theory. However, there has been no word from the doctor himself. But there are new developments in the story. Someone from the University of Eastern Illinois has told me on the condition of anonymity that Dr. Hartford's original conclusion was not, 'What We Were is now Who We Are' but indeed, 'What We Should Have Been isn't What We were so 'Being Now' isn't 'What We Are'.

Leslie: What else did the source tell you?

Mark: I'll tell you Leslie, it seems like 'cold fusion' all over again. This source is convinced that professor Hartford has lost certain nuances as to the conjugation of the verb to be, and has left the University without any choice but to reprimand him.

Leslie: But Mark isn't being what we were the whole part of having once been?

Mark: Yes Leslie, but my source's contention is that having once been precludes any situation of now being. And they say Dr. Hartford knew this. They say he knew it and published his report anyway.

Leslie: Indeed a disturbing conclusion if proved true. We'll go to break now... no, I've been told that we will go back to the Forbes institute where the distinguished Dr. Householder has been joined by milkman John Avery. Let's start with you Mr. Avery since you haven't been on yet. What about the assertion of what was, was, and what is, is, because of what has been?

John: Well, if it were spoilt, then it's gonna be spoilt. If it aint spoilt, then you don't really know if it's spoilt or not. The best thing to do is to check the little date on the top. That is, if it's been in the refrigerator the whole time. If it's been sittin' in the sun all day there ain't no tellin'.

Dr. Householder: I think what my colleague is trying to say is that if what was, was, and then it doesn't necessarily hold a bond on what is. How could anyone assert that having been is the same as now being?

Leslie: Does this reflect your line of thought Mr. Avery?

John: Hell, if you can't read the date, just give it the sniff test. The old snoot sure knows the difference between what is and was.

Leslie: Thank you both for being on the program. Now, for political insight, we go to our political commentator, Bill Shneeder. Bill, what can we expect as political fallout from all this?

Bill: Well Leslie, Dr. Hartford's definition of the verb to be is certainly Clintonesque if anything. Both major candidates have refused comment so far, but sources close to me say the Democratic candidate is leaning toward the 'what was is now' stance. Not exactly aligning himself with Dr. Hartford, but not denying it either. The Republican National Committee, however, has taken the bold move of issuing a statement saying, and I quote, "Our great nation wasn't founded on the notion of what was, but instead on the visionary leadership of what will be." Leslie?

Leslie: Bill is there any indication as to how "being" "is" and "was" is going to play out in the polls?

Bill: Our poll numbers indicate that the public is a bit confused on the matters of "is" and "was" but that likely voter's support "being" by a whopping margin of two to one.

Leslie: Thank you Bill. After a short break we'll be back with more on our main story of the day, "Wild goats: Ruminants or reprobates?"

White Stove,
White Christmas

The old, white oven sat in the alley behind Joseph's house for as long as he could remember. Every day on his walk home from school, he would inspect it as if for the first time. The door would come open and odd smells would come out. Depending on the season, and temperature outside, a different odor would emanate each time the old spring hinged door was opened. Using the small, stained window on the front of the dilapidated unit, Joseph always looked inside the oven to see if there was something there before pulling down the rusted chrome handle of the door. There was never anything there.

One day, while walking home from school, Joseph noticed new graffiti on the old white oven. It said 'white power.' Joseph thought it was ironic that on a white porcelain stove, made in America, that someone would spray in black spray paint the words 'white power.' The words were crudely drawn and came over the little window. He leaned down to look into the window but could no longer see the interior of the stove. He had a drive to correct the situation. No-one should cover his window with anything. He went home, got his mother's finger nail polish remover and a small rag, and went back to clean off the small window. It took some scrubbing, but it worked.

For some reason, cleaning off the small window brought back memories to Joseph. There, in the dark alley, Joseph knelt in front of the small stove stroking at the little window. Ignoring sirens from the dark street outside, he faded into memories of his fourteen years of life. He shook into a daydream and it was strong and vivid. Staring into the little glass window he could see many things. His first memorable Christmas was one that came to the forefront.

It was December twenty fourth and his mother and father were going through their normal machinations of screeching at each other. The little window, in this desolate alley, in the dark, glowed as bright as any television screen for the young eyes. Memories glistened in the little grease stained window. The wind blew papers and leaves over the small oven but Joseph didn't notice. He was focused on the little window of the oven, memories, and visions came.

The drama between his mother and father became so fierce while he was opening presents, designed for his pleasure, he finally retreated out of the room with the shabby Christmas tree, needles carpeting the floor, went out the door, and into the front lawn. He looked in the little window on the front part of his house, where he could view the lights of the disheveled tree inside. There, he could hear his parents yell, but could see his reflection of himself shaking and crying on Christmas day. There he was, with the wrapping of one of his packages clutched in two fists. He saw himself sitting there and suddenly felt separated from the actions happening around him. It was very cold outside, but all he could feel was the warmth of opening his presents.

He had gone out to where his father had spent hours lacing the pine tree near the road with lights. They were bright green, red, yellow and orange. They were of the large variety. Nothing his father did was small. There were big trucks, big parties, big pools, and big welts on his hindquarters from the big belt. It was a point of order, Joseph thought, to be big in all things. He climbed up into the big tree, nestled himself amongst the big lights, and listened to the yelling in the house. The lights were warm and he pressed them near to his face. Breathing into the lights he said, "There is some warmth in Christmas, isn't there?" The cold breeze whipped through the tree. "Feel the breeze and the cold," he whispered. He sucked in the warm air from the lights, caressed the lights, felt the rough bark of the tree on his back, then heard his father yell at him to come down and come inside the house. He wondered if the big belt would be waiting for him.

The little white oven turned off its window as Joseph turned off the memory. He stroked with a flat hand at the cold stained window wondering whether to try and turn it back on or not. A memory came to him as he stood in the cold windy alley while the stained window stared back at him. He stood, turned to walk, but the memory followed him. The haunting, illuminating memory was that of an old man who was dying of skin cancer. This dying man was living, at the time of his memory, next door to his house. The old man caught Joseph stationing himself in his front yard to throw eggs at trick-or-treaters on Halloween night. The old man pulled the carton of eggs gently from Joseph's arm and let out a tired wheeze. As clear as it had been said a few years ago, the voice of the old man rippled in his ears, "Joseph," the old man said kindly, face scarred with surgery, thin white hair blowing in the breeze, "the only way to know what's wrong is to know what's right. You know this is wrong, so do what is right." Joseph knelt back down in front of the little window to watch the memory.

The old man died the week before Christmas. Joseph was compelled by his parents to go to the funeral, though he didn't want to go. He was very fond of the old man but didn't want to go because he was fiercely afraid of death. The funeral was that of an open casket and Joseph could see the poor, embalmed, cancer ridden carcass lying there passively. There were very few people at the funeral and he wondered who would come to visit him in the casket. The lowering of the casket terrified Joseph as he wondered how people could get to him and visit. He had liked to visit with the old man and wondered if he could make his way there and talk. A ten year old Joseph walked to the edge of the dirty, hollowed out gravesite; casket already lowered and whispered, "Merry Christmas. I'll try and learn what's right."

Joseph stood up from the small white stove, felt another cold breeze come across the back of his neck, and remembered it was Christmas Eve. As he started his rambling, reluctant, slow amble home, thoughts of Christmas Eve's past came to him. There was the screeching of his parents, a dearth of presents under the tree, and going to bed crying. He wondered if the old man could have a pleasant time up in Heaven while he was in such misery here on earth. Mom and dad would be angry that he was late. They would also be angry if he was early so he really didn't mind the time.

Small pieces of white paper crossed his path with the wind as he exited the dirty alley. To his left, he could see flames coming out of a barrel and a small crowd of disheveled homeless men trying to warm themselves. He wondered at how one could become like this; starving for warmth, comfort and food on Christmas Eve. The men were mumbling things to each other as Joseph walked by. They held their hands over the flaming barrel, rubbing them together from time to time. They each had on frayed knit caps to protect from the cold, were unshaven, and wore layers of an assortment of clothing long since destroyed by a previous owner. Joseph thought of it as a uniform of sorts. Each of the disheveled men looked eerily similar.

"Yeah," said one of the men, a large black man with many teeth missing, "I've spent years of my life devoted to the church. But if I want a meal, then I gots to go listen to some little volunteer tell me about Jesus. These young, little bastards are so hung up on Jesus they forgot about being Christian. Damn, I'm hungry and drunk but not immoral."

A wizened, small old white man pulled a bottle out of his jacket and extended it to the black man. "Calculator," he said to the black man, knowing his penchant for numbers, "everyone knows They took the Christ out of Christmas a long time ago. It's all about material things man. Jesus chased people out a temple for having money. But people spend money and say it's for Christmas while we starve. Now give me my bottle back"

The pace toward home for Joseph slowed while moving past the burning barrel and he found a tear exiting his eye as he listened to the homeless men. After he passed the small, warming inferno, he picked up the pace and faded in memory back to his cold, lonely stove as he neared home. He wished he would have stayed longer, kneeling down and wondering what other memories it would have bestowed. There were places in his young memory where he wanted to go, but was afraid to go there by himself. The little oven, he was convinced, would have helped him go where he had fear.

He saw that his father was sleeping on the couch when he opened the door of his small, disheveled house, and there was an empty bottle of brandy which lay by his father's slumbering side. The stench of his odor filled the room. Joseph looked around for his mother, wondering what sort of horrid verbal abuse was to come. He could take the physical abuse from his father, but, somehow, the verbal abuse from his mother struck into him like a hatchet into a dry piece of wood. There were days when this brutal language would not stop. Talking about how lazy, stupid, and inferior Joseph was to others had become a cottage industry to his mother. Joseph only cared because he cared for his mother. He cared for many reasons, one of which was watching her agonize with an acquaintance for hours and hours over a cup of coffee about how inadequate he was. He wished he could be better for her, but didn't know how.

When Joseph got deeper into the house, moving toward his bedroom, he saw his mother lying in the hallway, face down in a dress with yellow flowers on a red background. The dress had shifted up high enough to expose bare buttocks. She was still breathing but a bottle of her pills were still clutched tightly in her right hand. They were pain killers for one of her many psychosomatic disorders. She told her many doctors that she had anything which would get her more drugs. Sometimes she would overdo her self medication, then mix it with a little of dad's alcohol. The mix did not bode well for her ability to function. He watched the labored undulations of her breathing for a while and the sight brought tears to his eyes. He reached down to pull at her arm and whispered in her ear. "Mom, go to bed. Please go to bed." When she didn't respond, he pulled the dress down to try and find some dignity for his mother.

Joseph spent a lot of time thinking about things. He spent more time thinking when his parents were in this state. He would think about his lot in life and what he had learned in school. There weren't many friends as he was considered an odd-ball by most. He didn't mind not having friends as this made him immune from their taunting and he felt being an odd-ball had its benefits. Being disengaged was better than being engaged when it was so distasteful to do so. Anonymity soaked into him and sent him to regions of lark.

He found himself walking back to his little white oven. He was hungry and didn't care about one or the other of his parents waking to make supper. The fear of retribution from his parents, making a mess in the kitchen trying to cook something for him, was over riding his hunger. He thought he might find some food along the short walk. The homeless were digging in the dumpsters for food and seemed to be well fed. He leaned into one green, rust stained dumpster and found a crumpled bag from a fast food restaurant. Inside, were a half eaten burger and a few stale French fries. The new found food was cold, but palatable. It was very dark in the alley, but he sniffed at and felt for the food as he un-crumpled the bag

The little stove was there for him, illuminated slightly by a street light at the far end of the alley and he sat down in front of it, crossing his legs, munching the last of his stale French fries. Inside the little oven was a vision. It was different from the visions he was used to. Up to this point, the visions were exclusively reflections on what had been. This time, the vision had, for the first time, an audio and was not just about what he had seen or felt in life. It started out with what he knew. He saw his favorite teacher and he was talking about life. "Life," he said, "is a journey and not a destination." The grey bearded teacher adjusted his tie, as he always did at the beginning of class and continued. "There will come a time in everyone's life when things seem hopeless. But never lose hope. I've seen these days, but I know no-one should ever lose hope."

A shadow came over him. He looked up and saw a silhouette of a man standing between him and the street light beyond. "You got some place to stay little man?" said the shadowy figure. "We got some boxes and blankets down the way if you don't"

"No, I mean yes," said Joseph. "I have a place to stay. I just don't want to be there now."

"You do know it's Christmas Eve little feller. If you got a home, you should be there. Now go home and be there." He gauged the sour look on Joseph's face when he mentioned the word 'home'. "I'll bet there are all kinds of things waiting for you. There are all kinds of bad people walking around here. Don't stay too long." Then the homeless man turned toward the light and walked away. Before he turned the corner, he said over his shoulder, "I'll be here all night. I don't got no home to go to. If you need help, my name is Gypsy. Everyone down here knows me." Then waving a finger in the air he added, "Catch the wind while you can still breathe little man." Leaning back around the corner he added, "Little fellah, when life gets rough, you've just got to get smooth." With a nearly toothless smile he said, "Merry Christmas."

The little window came to life one more time, this time with complete fantasy. His bearded teacher was there and said, "Joseph, there are dimensions in the world. There is up, there is down and there is side to side. Einstein told us that there is a fourth dimension; that of the space time continuum. I believe, young man, that there is another dimension to reality in the universe. We live in a three dimensional world with an imperceptible fourth dimension around us. Think for a moment," he said stroking his stubbly white beard as he had always done, "if there is another dimension, just as imperceptible as the gravitational warping of the fabric of space, it could be one for the spiritual worlds.

"Think of this," the teacher went on, "we are in the dimensions of space and time but the dimension of the spiritual is could be as far outside of our perception as the curvature of space is." The lights inside the dirty window of the oven grew brighter as the teacher continued. "Just think, that outside of these four dimensions we call reality, that there are spiritual dimensions. I believe, with all my heart that these four dimensions are a dividing line of a sort. In the spiritual dimension, there needs to be delineations between heaven and hell. And here we are right between the two. If we could perceive this dividing line, we could reach out with one hand and touch Christ then we could reach out with the other and touch the devil. We, unbeknownst to all of us while living, and while acting out the comedy of life, are sandwiched in an instant between heaven and hell. If you have no morals, you can fall one way when you die. If you have led a moral life, you fall the other way and be able to stare at all of those who have fallen the wrong way. There, the evil people will be, as the bible says, begging for water. But there is no getting across the space time continuum to give them water even if you wanted to. The barrier of reality is there and you could never, under any circumstance get there. Jesus was the only entity born into flesh that passed across this barrier, from one side to the other. Fall into the correct and moral side Joseph." The light then went off and all that was left was a lonely stove, a cold windy alley, and a sad young man.

The walk home seemed much longer than usual. The distance wasn't up to a quarter mile, but now it seemed like miles and miles. He would do the right thing, he thought. Musing about doing the right thing and falling into the direction of heaven lessened the darkness of his mood. Some houses, in this disheveled neighborhood, had up some Christmas lights. Some had all white little lights, others had multi colored lights that clicked on and off at regular intervals. One house had a small nativity in the middle of the tiny front lawn. He paused to look at the illuminated head of baby Jesus in the would be manger. It was relatively bright as compared to the dark surroundings. Joseph knelt beside the erstwhile crib and queried out loud, "Dear Jesus, haven't I lived in hell long enough to be sure to fall into heaven one day? I will do the best I can. That's all I can do. Please don't let me fall into another hell."

His father was still on the couch, snoring gently. His mother had roused enough to get to the bed. The slight vibration of closing the door let more needles fall off the shabby tree. The needles showered the two presents under the tree. One was bought by him for his mother and father. He had trouble with the wrapping and couldn't get the ribbon to curl as he had seen others do stroking the scissors in rapid fashion along the left over ribbon. The gold ribbon lay limp on the small red package. He had mown lawns all summer to save up for a fancy picture frame his mother once told him she wanted. He squirreled away what money wasn't taken by his father for his booze, or what money was taken for drugs by his mother. The frame had a picture of a happy couple. He took it out and put in a picture of his mother and father who were smiling at their wedding.

Joseph started making some supper but had trouble finding food that wasn't spoiled in the refrigerator. The noise of his pots and pans rattling around roused his father. His father came into the kitchen with his stained t-shirt on, whitish hair unkempt and, without provocation, slapped Joseph very hard. "All this noise is going to wake your mother," he screamed at Joseph much louder than any noise the pots and pans were making. Then the unshaven father went back to his couch and took a swig from his half empty bottle.

After sneaking out the back door, Joseph felt a strange sense of guilt. His breath was frosty white in the cold air. His tears ran down his face and snot drooled down his face. He was supposed to do the right thing, he thought. But doing the right thing just didn't make sense to him. The cold alleyway was the most welcoming moment of this Christmas Eve. He stumbled in the dark to find his inanimate friend. Memories needed to fuel the good side of his mood. Reaching the end of the alley, he found that it was gone. The shock of his little white oven missing made him suddenly feel the cold with all intensity.

Crying, shaking, and moaning, Joseph bowed his head. He stayed there sobbing for quite some time, until he felt a hand pull on his shoulder. "Aw, little man. What are you crying about? You remember Gypsy, don't you?"

Joseph looked at the silhouette, illuminated from behind and gasped out, "They took my stove. They took my stove." He rubbed a sleeve across his drooling nose. "Who took it?"

Gypsy rubbed a hand gently over Joseph's head. "Little man," he said, "it wasn't your stove. It didn't work anyway. That's why it was tossed in this alley. Why don't you go home and enjoy Christmas. Hell, I've been thrown away and towed away and I own myself. That didn't make me mad. Don't be sad about something you don't own being gone. I guess that's why I got nothing. I don't have to worry about missing anything. I don't know who took this stove, but I do know it was almost as worthless as me. Now go home and enjoy Christmas."

"I hate Christmas. I hate my family," yelled Joseph with tears starting to flow again.

A big stout arm wrapped around Joseph's shoulder. "Young man," Gypsy said. "Come on with me. I got some things to show you."

As they both walked to the end of the alley, the street light illuminated them both. Joseph, for the first time, could see how disheveled Gypsy was. He had on a thin green coat, a torn sweater and his face was unshaven. Gloves with the end of the fingers torn off adorned his hands. His boots had no shoelaces and made a scratching sound as he guided Joseph along. Other things came to Joseph as they walked: the stench Gypsy had emanating from him and a decided limp.

"Now, I've seen you in that alley talking to that little stove," Gypsy said to Joseph. "That's okay. I talk to things all the time. Hell, one time, in the heat of summer, I used to talk to a fire hydrant. I would ask it to cool me off with its water." He stopped his ambling walk and looked to Joseph. "Do you know what that damn fire hydrant used to say to me?"

Joseph shook his head and said, "I don't know."

"Easy answer," Gypsy said with a yellow toothed grin illuminated by the yellow street light, "that fire hydrant always said 'No!'. As hot as I was, and as long as I stared at it and as long as I talked it was always 'No!'" Pulling Joseph tighter under his arm he added, "Come on. I've got something to show you."

Rounding the next corner, in the adjacent alley from where the stove had been the light was brighter than the alley of the stove and Joseph could make out a series of cardboard boxes with legs sticking out of them. He could hear the gentle snoring of the men and women camped out there. There were shopping carts, pieces of clothing and wadded up wrappers of fast food. Joseph took in the scene and felt like running, but didn't.

"This is my home, little man," Gypsy said. "I don't care how bad your house is, it ain't as bad as this. Now come on, I got something to show you in my house." He grinned his yellow grin again and led Joseph to his box.

It was a large box and the third one on the left in the barely illuminated alley. Gypsy crawled inside and motioned for Joseph to follow. Joseph was hesitant and let his eyes get accustomed to the dim light before advancing. He knelt down at the opening and said, "Gypsy, I'm kind of afraid."

"There's never a reason to be afraid of Gypsy," Gypsy said. "Ask anyone here." He came out of the box and pointed back and forth to all the other boxes in the alley. "Seriously, ask anyone here."

Joseph noticed something in Gypsy's hand and asked, "What's that?"

Gypsy gave his yellowish grin again and pulled himself into a seated position legs crossed, and looked into Joseph's face. "Young man," he started, "you just think you got a rotten holiday. I think the difference could only be the state of the human mind. Me? I'm going to get a good Christmas. I'm going to get a meal at the shelter and get warm for a while. You want to know what's in my hand?"

"Yes sir," Joseph said.

Laughing, Gypsy said, "No-one has called me 'sir' in years. Just call me Gypsy. Now here is what is in my hand." He opened his hand and there was a small doll. It was a dirty cloth replica of a reindeer. It had on a red sash and green boots. "Here," Gypsy said. "You take it. It sounds like you need someone to talk to and I talk to Rudolph all the time. He's a good listener. I know he ain't got a red nose but that's Rudolph for sure."

"I can't take this," said Joseph, "if it's your friend."

"Oh no," said Gypsy extending the small doll to Joseph, "You take this. This thing will never break. No-one can take it away. You can talk to it forever. Your little stove might be in a warm home right now being fixed with someone else to talk to. You never know. Hold this close, when you are lonely at night, and sometimes Rudolph will talk back.

Someday, when you don't need Rudolph, and when you have people to talk to, give him to someone else lonely and they can talk to him too. This is my Christmas present to you. Now go home and get some sleep and get ready for Christmas."

Joseph took the small, wobbly doll and said to Gypsy, "Thank you. Is there anything I can get for you? Won't you be lonely now without Rudolph?"

"No little man," another yellow grin showing itself. "Your company on Christmas Eve was all the company I could wish for. Now, Merry Christmas little man, Merry Christmas."

Heaven is Overrated

Avenues of thought crisscrossed his conscious like a crazy freeway interchange or maybe more like the mangled web of a spider. How does one decipher the blitz of incoming information put out by the crazy world and then be expected to find the way home? When there are no road signs, no road maps, and no-one to get advice from as to where to go, how was it possible to divine the path in the life he wanted? He had ridden a motorcycle through London, Paris, Budapest, Vienna, Berlin, Prague and Madrid. In all these places, he had always had a notion of where he was. No matter how convoluted the adventure, he always knew he would find out where he was and a way back. But in traveling the emotional roads of his life, he often felt completely lost. There were no maps, no signs for direction, and no-one to trust for direction. Fear of indecision at his necessary action frequently brought into the harbor of his mind a well loaded freighter of paranoia which would come to berth against his mental state. This set him into fits of fear and suspicion against others.

When he believed he finally knew where he was physically and emotionally, he felt it was too late to get back. His life was a shambles and his mind a tornado of swirling ideas, but, for some reason, he recognized the curb he was sitting on. This gave him some comfort.

Crying didn't mitigate anything anymore and it didn't help him back to the place where he had started and thought he had to be, so he tried not to cry anymore. William, the short chubby confused man he was, sat on the curb and analyzed his position. There were noisy vehicles roaring inches from his splayed feet. Dust from the dirty route coated him. The dust caused him to think about the dust from his childhood home. His father would drive down the long dirt road, screech to a halt, and send a cloud of dust over the young son who was running out to greet him. As soon as the ridiculously loud pick-up shut off the father would get out and throw his arms around the little boy. William wished there was someone now who would emerge through the dust of this noisy road to throw their arms around him. As much as he tried to hold back, the memories of his old, bespectacled, father with his bibbed overalls on exiting the old rusted truck to hug him caused another tear to exit his eye.

While lingering in his childhood daydream, William stood and dusted off his backside. He felt the coarse wind of a passing semi-truck and trailer and squint his eyes and held his breath until the cloud of dust swept past him. The large vehicle went down the road spitting out a brown vapor to either side as it moved like a boat sending out a wake in what had been calm water. He put a hand up to the side of his face and tried once more not to reminisce. Yet the thoughts were there and as he started to walk down the sidewalk to no-where the memories took over his being and went with him.

Shimmering calm water reflecting the brilliant sun stung his eyes. The little boat made ripples as it moved and these gentle undulations of water could be seen roiling out a hundred yards with the wake. The lake was empty except for the little aluminum boat. The two erstwhile fishermen had on caps with the obligatory fly fishing hooks stuck in them. Even though they were only going bait fishing today, the hats made for good decoration. William's father had over two dozen hooks in his hat but William only had six or seven. They only caught patches of bright pink skin that day on the empty lake but William found a very fond memory. When this fishing trip was over, after returning to their respective homes, William got a phone call from his mother. His father had died of a heart attack. That fishing trip was the last time he saw his father alive.

A voice shook William out of his wandering memory. "Dude, you got any change?" said the voice coming from his right side. The voice originated from a disheveled young man with long greasy hair and wearing a torn blue t-shirt that had printed on it in red the letters GOTOHELL. William got up and started a brisk pace to nowhere.

The young man matched the pace with William and repeated, "Dude, do you have any change? Like, I need some money. Like, you look like a man of means. I'm like an unemployed Chemist and down on my luck."

William stopped his forward progress and asked the grubby young man, "Are you 'like' an unemployed Chemist, or *are* you an unemployed Chemist."

"Hey, why are you being so nosey?" the young man asked with puckered lips. "All I wanted was some change. Do you got some or not?"

The noise of the street seemed to fade from William's ears after the question ended. "I'm not being nosey," William said, "I'm just repeating what you said and I don't believe you about being a Chemist. But I've got to get going so you don't need to respond."

William started to walk away when the young, filthy man said, "Dude, do you got any change you can spare or not?"

William patted his pockets with an irritated expression then inverted them exposing the white liner and some lint. "I don't have any change." He paused for a second then added, "What would that 'change' do for you anyway? If I had fifty cents to give you, you'd still be a bum and you would probably just spend it on booze. No amount of money would actually make you 'change', now go and get some help and stop panhandling."

"Oh dude, nice double entendre there. By the way, you can't get booze on fifty cents," the young man said with a smile. "If I could buy booze for fifty cents I'd be drunk all the time. But I can't so I don't. Dude, like, where are you going? You sure you don't got any change?"

"If I had money," William snapped, "I'd be taking a taxi and get away from people like you."

"Oh come on dude. What do you know about people like me? Is where you are going a place where you can get some change? I ain't a bad guy. All I want is a little bit of money. Then I could get something to eat. Hell, a guy dressed like you could spare a couple of bucks." He then tugged at the lapel of William's jacket. "See, look at that jacket. That suit must have cost one thousand dollars."

"Don't touch me," William snapped, pushing the young man's hand away. "This suit, for your information cost me fifteen hundred dollars. I don't need your greasy hands on it. I worked for it." William cocked his head to one side and added with a sneer, "Do you know what work is? I went to school, got a degree, so that I could get a job to earn money to buy fancy suits; suits that don't need filthy hands on them."

The young man kept pace with William down the noisy and dusty boulevard and said, "I told you, I've got a degree."

William stopped his walk and turned to look at the torn, GOTOHELL, t-shirt and asked, "And what kind of degree might we have?"

"Dude," said the young man, sticking both hands toward William, quivering unnaturally. "I told you. I don't know what 'we've' got but I've got a Chemistry degree. It was like really hard to get, but I got it."

Having the thought of this disheveled creature seen in front of him as having a degree in Chemistry had William stop and sent his jaw drooping. "What?" said William, "You're trying to tell me that you have a degree in Chemistry?"

"No dude, I'm not *trying* to tell you, I'm telling you. I've got a Chemistry degree. And it wasn't one of that wimpy Bachelor of Arts kind of degree; it was a Bachelor of Science. Like the real deal dude."

Painting a smirk on his face, William said, "At least you're not pretending to be a Vietnam Veteran. And pray tell, young man, what was your most difficult class at your prestigious university while getting this B.S. in Chemistry?"

"Whoa dude, that's easy. It was Physical Chemistry. They threw in thermodynamics, but my lab partner used to call it thermo-god-damn-ics. I had a real weird professor for Inorganic Chemistry which made that difficult too. But dude, P. Chem.'s lab was just cool. It was the class work that made it unbearable. Like who needs to know the energy levels for a particle in a box? I had to learn about a theoretical particle in a theoretical box and had to pretend I understood and cared. It just got too ridiculous. Who needs to know this crap? And why did I spend so much time trying to learn it?"

The smirk flew off William's face and made a crash landing in the realm of bewilderment. With jaw drooping more than before, he recovered to say, "I'm beginning to believe you actually do have a degree. But what the hell are you doing on the street, in ragged clothes, and smelling like urine?"

"Dude," the young fellow said while sniffing at his shirt, "I didn't pee myself. This dude we call Buddy, a short snotty drunk, pissed on me while I was sleeping. Do you know what it's like waking up under a golden shower? I punched that little freak right in the balls."

William shook his head back and forth. "I can't say I do know or understand what that is like, I mean that shower thing. But if you have such an honorable degree, why don't you have a job?"

A burst of laughter came out of the smelly man's face. "Honorable? That's a good one." he said, trying to stifle his laughter. "When did having student loans out the ass for a profession that pays you slave wages become 'honorable'? Hell, I make more money sleeping in a box than working. At least I break even and the loan people can't find me." He then got a quizzical smile on his face, revealing stained teeth, and started singing while doing a little dance. "Momma don't let your babies grow up to be Chemists. They'll work in labs they don't understand. The EPA will crawl up his butthole and make him so sore he'll not be able to stand." He gave out another giggle when he finished his tune and then added, "Dude, I think all my professors were graduates of the Stanley Milgram School of inflicting punishment. Someone told them to inflict this painful worthless crap on us so they kept doing it to fulfill their sense of duty to authority." The young man squint his eyes, clinched his fists and in a pleading voice added, "Zap, zap, zap, oh please stop professor, zap, zap. I think I'm going to die. I swear I'll learn what Crystal Field Theory is all about even though I know I'll never use it. Oh, wrong answer, zap, zap, zap."

Stopping his brisk pace William turned to the man shadowing his walk and asked, "What is your name young man?"

"Well, it's not Milgram for sure. But I believe my mother bestowed on me the title of Theodore Michael Birchmont. Most everyone calls me Ted which I prefer. Well, technically Birchmont was already there so she didn't add that. That was my father's sur-name. My mother's maiden name was Sequel, which always made me think of why she didn't cash in on the irony of changing her name back. Think of it: the sequel of Sequel. Do you get it?"

"Yes, I get it Ted. My name is William. As much as you might like to believe it, not everyone is stupid. And just because you have a degree doesn't make what you are doing with your life smart." William gave out a sigh. "You mentioned that you needed something to eat. I can buy you lunch and then you can tell me more about why you are out here on the street and not being more productive."

"Man, I thought you didn't have any money."

"I've got credit cards Ted. We can eat all we want on that." He pointed to a plastic card produced from his wallet.

"You asked me if I could be productive?" said Ted as they resumed their brisk walk. "Hell dude, what's your definition of being productive? I do more good for the people around here and humanity in general than I ever would by pumping samples into an instrument in some sterile lab. I consider that productive. What do you consider productivity?"

"I would," started William, "consider productivity to be some activity that produces something and retrieving the reward for doing so such as remuneration and material goods. I work ten hours a day six days a week. Hard work will reap rewards."

"Ha," laughed Ted. "So let me get this straight. You spend all your time behind a desk, buying a house you only see when you're getting to bed, and spend your spare time shopping for toys you will never have time to use. This sounds absolutely wonderfully productive to me.

"Look dude, I'm not trying to be rude but what I'm trying to say is that I'll never trade freedom for convenience. It's all a question of priorities. I'll never trade being poor to having to slave for money and things. People, like you, assume that I'm miserable. These last couple of years, here on the street, hasn't always been comfortable, but I wouldn't trade these days for all the caviar swimming in the Volga River or the fanciest heated house. Hell, everything I got is free and anything I want I get from people who waste their lives working themselves to the end of their days. I consider giving money to me a conscience salve of sorts for these poor working stiffs. Letting them give me money is my way of letting them feel good about wasting their lives."

"Ted, when your belly is full and your hunger is sated, then you can tell me all about the wasted living I have done by earning money so that I can buy you lunch."

"Dude, you're missing the point. You don't have to feed me. I would appreciate it if you did but I think sometimes that sating an empty belly is easier than sating an empty soul. Hell, I can go dumpster diving and get something to eat and sate my hunger. You can't go dumpster diving to sate what you need for the soul."

"Hey," William hissed, grabbing Ted by his upper arm and yanking him to a stop. "Don't judge me. I don't need any crap from a homeless man who has farcical aspirations to moral authority. If you want lunch,

I'll buy it. But I don't need the reincarnation of Jean Paul Sartre, who is now a street bum, teaching me the existentialist road to true enlightenment. Now shut your mouth, or stay hungry." He turned loose of Ted's arm and started again on his brisk walk.

"Dude," said Ted, struggling to keep up. "I guess I'm messing this all up. All I wanted to do was to make you happier. I can go hungry. I've done that many times before and will again. So not buying me a meal is no threat to me. But you are obviously in threat to something. It's not every day you find a dude in a fifteen hundred dollar suit sitting on the curb and sulking. Something is bugging you in a big, buggy sort of way. Dude, happiness is the only thing I can afford to give to anyone. Happiness, I really think, has value beyond any material good that you can order or take off the shelf. Then you will have to worry about whatever you bought breaking or being stolen. A television can be stolen, but happiness can't be taken if you are right in here." Ted thumped a fist over his heart to emphasize his comment and to indicate where it was to be 'right' in.

William stayed silent until they entered a restaurant which they found along the walk. Thoughts of the things Ted had said bounced unwillingly and involuntarily in his skull. The remembrance of sitting on the curb came to him in full force and the depression he had been feeling swamped over him like a rogue wave. As they entered the café and were ushered to a booth with cracked green vinyl seats, the nightmare that had left him lost on a street corner came back to his mind in a flash. He was losing his job, his wife was leaving him and he couldn't remember where he lived or where he had worked. "Where was life without living?" he thought. He would spend the time and money to be with this homeless, erstwhile philosopher then try and find his way home. "There must be a way to find my way back home."

"What did you say?" asked Ted. William hadn't realized that his private thoughts had actually exited his mouth in an audible fashion. "Dude, I've go no home and I don't worry about it. Like the Janis Joplin song said, having nothing left is nothing left to lose. If you can forget where you live, it probably wasn't worth remembering. Dude, when you want to remember where you live, you will remember. But until then, uninspired by some sort of affection to remember where it is, there really ain't no reason to worry about it."

The waitress, a frumpy looking older woman with black horn

rimmed glasses and hair pulled up into a bun, plopped down the two cups of coffee ordered by William. She pulled out her ordering pad from the oversized pockets of her light blue smock and then pulled a pen from behind her ear. She did the inexplicable ritual of licking the tip of the pen then said, "What's in it for you guys today?"

"Well," started Ted, "I really didn't want any coffee. Do you got beer or wine?"

The frumpy waitress smacked her lips and said, "We have both. What would you like?"

"Wow, I'll take one of each," said Ted. "Give me a house red wine and a light beer." With a wide smile and a point of the finger toward William, all the while looking to the waitress, he added, "I'm climbing on the gravy train today sweetheart. So don't be shy filling up that goblet and make sure the beer is cold."

The waitress leaned to pick up the coffee mug but Ted restrained her by grabbing the mug with both hands. "You can leave that," he said. "There's no sense in tossing out clean liquid. Honey, you can't believe what you will drink when you're thirsty. Today, I don't want to be thirsty."

The frumpy waitress stood up straight, gave a bland look to the smelly homeless man and said, "I'm not your sweetheart and I'm not your honey. Now, are you ready to order?"

"Yeah," said Ted with some enthusiasm, ignoring the woman's distaste, "I'll have the chicken fried steak with hash browns, a side order of fries, a side of onion rings, and when that's done I'll have a slice of your cherry pie with whipped cream."

The woman stopped scribbling the order and turned her stern countenance to William. "I'll just have the cream cheese bagel," he said. The waitress picked up their menus and went to the opening to the kitchen and clipped the order onto the rotating metal ring which was used by the chefs to keep a proper queue for how and when the orders were placed. She tapped on a little pushbutton bell which indicated a new order had been posted.

"At least I never had to live like this," Ted said while waggling an index finger toward the frumpy waitress. "That poor woman just exudes misery. Hell, almost as much misery as you have on the halo around you. But yours is more palpable. Yours is more mysterious. This woman obviously wants more and thinks by working hard she'll get what she wants. You, on the other hand, seem to have gotten a lot of things, which seem to be what you wanted, but still are miserable. Me? I've got what I want which is nothing in the material field but everything I want in the spiritual field."

"Would you stop lecturing me, please," gasped out William. "I'm just in a lull here. You pride yourself on spreading happiness so why do you kick a guy when he's down? Yes, I could probably find a way to position myself in living in a way to make things better. Yes, I could do that. But you have no empathy for people who try and make the economy run. Have you ever thought about the sacrifice people go through to keep people warm, safe, and dry in the winter?"

"What day is it William?" asked Ted.

"Oh Christ," replied William, rattling his head back and forth, "You don't even know what day it is?" He put his elbows on the table and held out two palms directed toward Ted. "What day do you think it is?"

"Oh, I know what day it is. It's Saturday."

"And when you do nothing and are proud of it, why do you care what day it is?"

Just then the waitress brought out the beer and wine. Ted thanked her then reached into a little white container which had the sugar packets. He took one little packet out, tore off the top then dumped the contents into his coffee. "Saturday is significant for only one reason. You told me you worked six days a week. Since you're not working now, today, on Saturday, I doubt you actually work six days a week."

"I took a day off, okay?"

"Why did you take a day off?"

"Oh great," said William, starting to rub a hand across his face. "Now you have gone from the philosopher Jean Paul Sartre to the psychoanalyst Sigmund Freud. I'm not lying on a couch so that you can ask me reflexive questions. Who are you going to be reincarnated into next? Are you going to become Steven Hawking and tell me about the Cosmos? Or maybe you will become Winston Churchill and tell me about the political hubris of the day? Are you trying to become the subject of a book about multiple personalities? Will you then change your name from Ted to Eve?"

"Dude, like, when it comes to reincarnation, if you believe that stuff, I'm pretty sure you've got to be dead first before you can come back. The last I checked, Steven Hawking ain't dead yet. So your understanding of the cosmos will have to wait. Anyway, maybe old Winnie, that's what I call Mr. Churchill, will stop by for a visit and I can tell you all about British politics. If he doesn't stop by, and I can't channel into his demised conciseness, it won't bother me because I don't care about British politics and I'm sure you don't either. But, even if he showed up, old Winnie wouldn't be able to tell me why you ain't at work. The reason for you not being at work is for you to tell me. Maybe if I morphed into Nostradamus I would figure it out."

"It's none of your business why I didn't go to work."

"Alright," said Ted while shaking his head up and down, "I will channel the dead soul of Nostradamus and find out for myself." He then squint his eyes, stretched out his arms and placed one hand back to front on the other and began swirling his thumbs around as if the hands were swimming. "Om, I see a man who is being fired from his job. Om, I see a man named William who has marital problems. I see him searching for meaning in life, even if it means getting consultation from a urine soaked bum." After a big sigh Ted dropped his hands and opened his eyes. "I have been released from the spirit of Nosty. That's what Nostradamus wants me to call him." He finished off with a maniacal laugh which caused snot to exit his nose.

William smacked his hands on the table. "You don't know anything about me. I don't care what Nosty says, everything you said was wrong. I have a job. I have a lovely wife. I, I," he stammered, just before tears exited his eyes. He lowered his head onto the table and began to sob.

The frumpy waitress was standing by the table and Ted finally noticed her. She had loads of food on her arms and she had a scowl on her face. She looked at the sobbing William and said, "Hell, our food isn't that bad." She started placing the plates carefully on the table. "You haven't even tasted this stuff yet. And even the worst bagel isn't worth crying over; now your friend here, when he eats this chicken fried steak, and those greasy onion rings, he will have a legitimate reason to cry. Then there will be the sprint to the toilet. Crying is better than blowing a hole in your shorts. Maybe you're crying about his scent." She gave Ted a sour look then spun on her heels and started back toward her counter of complete control where she went behind, plopped an elbow on it and cuffed a hand under her chin.

"Dude," Ted said reaching out to tap the sobbing man on the

shoulder, "let me tell you a story. There was this dude named Charles Dickens who started out a book with the line 'It was the best of times it was the worst of times'. Every day I live, it has the best and the worst. What keeps me from despair is that I only think about the best of times and push the worst of times down the river Styx. I'm sure you have had good times, funny times, and times that just don't matter. I ain't no Sigmund whatever, I ain't got a couch, but you still can tell me about one of your good times."

William's head slowly came off the coffee table. He looked at Ted then pulled a napkin out of the dispenser and blew his nose. He pulled out another and handed it to Ted. "Blow your nose Ted," he said, "it's drooling." Ted blew his nose and then resumed stuffing his face.

"You want to know one of my good times?" asked William.

"Hmph," grunted Ted with a mouth stuffed with French fries.

"Well, I'll tell you a good memory," said William with eyes red from crying, "as long as you tell me a good memory that you have. Can we agree on that?"

"Hmph," grunted Ted, this time his mouth plugged with onion rings.

"Okay," said William, pushing his bagel to one side. "I've got a story for you." He took a sip of coffee and continued. "When I was in high school I worked at a feedlot. It may seem strange sounding, but there was a thing people called a packing shed which boxed up cantaloupes next to this giant feedlot. When it was late at night, I would squeeze through the gate to the packing shed and pick up some cantaloupes. It was really hot, even at night, and the packing shed had a huge tub of chilled water where the cantaloupes remained floating. I used to splash that cold water into my face and onto the back of my neck. I would usually take only one cantaloupe, sit on the other side of the fence and eat it. The cold flesh of that melon tasted so good. I wasn't really stealing, because I would pick out melons designated as culls which were too ripe to pack. The culls were considered waste. I can't eat cantaloupe anymore. Those cold, over ripe melons, eaten on a hot summer's night, left behind anything in flavor and sweetness than I ever have had in a melon of any kind since."

"Shtounds cool, dude," Ted mumbled out with a wad of chicken fried steak in his mouth. "I could usthe a cold melon now." The chomping went on, and so did the story by William.

"The only thing I regret about this whole mélange of memory was that there was this one regretful night when I pushed into the gate. I took four cantaloupes instead of just one. I ate only one of them but took the other three up into the grain tower. It was about eighty feet tall and was close to the road. I climbed up the ladder to the top of that grain tower holding the last three cantaloupes. Cars intermittently came by and I had the intention of doing something when I started climbing the tower. I was going to throw those cantaloupes at passing cars.

"It was a long throw, but I thought it would be hilarious, for some reason, to throw a cantaloupe at a car moving down the road. I was working the night shift so there wasn't a lot to do and I had plenty of time to wait for the next vehicle. When the first car came, I heaved the first melon and it missed by a long shot. I hadn't lead the trajectory sufficiently. After a few minutes, another car came along and I sent the next cantaloupe with the lead time in mind. It missed the car by inches, but I was still having fun. It was, to that time, the most exhilarating time of my life. I had to wait quite a while for the next vehicle to come along. When the lights of the car came into my Norden bombsight, I launched the last cantaloupe. The trajectory was perfect and I could tell I had success from the moment it left my hand. I followed that orb all the way down through the dim lighting of the front of the feedlot. When it hit the car, square on the hood, I was in ecstasy. Then the car stopped and red and blue lights came on the top of what happened to be a sheriff's cruiser.

"I dropped flat on my belly to the metal deck of the tower when the sheriff's spotlight started sweeping the area. I was trying to keep quiet but it was difficult as I was laughing so hard."

Scratching at the top of his greasy scalp, Ted asked, "Who's Norden?"

"What?" hissed out William, sounding more like he was clearing his throat than speaking. "I just told you a story you were asking for and all you want to know is who Norden is."

"Dude, what's the problem? Does everyone but me know who Norden is? Have I been missing something?" He jammed another wad of French fries into his mouth and continued. "I think it is germane to the story to know who he is. Don't dis me for wanting to understand what you've said. I'm just trying to be polite. The conveyance of understanding is the boulevard to enlightenment. All you got to do dude is coast and you'll get to spirit ease. It don't cost you nothin' and you don't need no gas. You've got to start soon though. I've been coasting for two years now and I still ain't seen the Promised Land."

William put his head back on the table, let out a groan and said, "Norden was an inventor. He invented a way to judge where bombs were dropped during World War II. It was a device to aid the pilots and bombardiers in hitting their targets. I wish they were dropping bombs on this café right now. And stop talking with your mouth full."

"Dude, you've got, like, morbid thoughts. No wonder you're depressed. Think about good things. Like, I think about the flowers in the park and how they smell. I think about the times I've scored an uneaten hamburger in a bag. I think about the time I pulled all those kittens out of the sewer drain and put them in a bag to take them down to the SPCA. I don't like to think about bombs and bombing and the terror it puts into the people who survive. I would rather die of thirst in the desert than bomb people. Why do *you* think about bombing people?"

"I wasn't thinking about bombing anyone. I was thinking about a cantaloupe I threw at a cop car years ago. The Norden bombsight was just a reference, a metaphor for what I was feeling years ago. I'm not going to get into a Stuka, put whistles on bombs to terrorize civilians, then drop them and strafe Polish civilians. Is it sinking in yet?"

Waggling an index finger at William and with a smile Ted said, "I think someone has had a breakthrough here. Let's just agree, here and now, that you have forsaken Norden's evil blasting of women and children."

"Oy, yo, yo," gasped out William, while raising his head. "Listen to me you imbecile, Norden never bombed anyone. He was the inventor of the air guidance system that delivered the bombs. I don't know the man personally, but I'm pretty damn sure he never dropped a bomb on anyone. Capice?"

"So, what you are telling me," said Ted, while tapping a finger on the side of his face, "is that if you invent something that kills people, you have no complicity in the fact it is used to kill people." He then shoved the last of his gravy covered chicken fried steak in his mouth in a huge bite.

"Okay, let's take Alfred Nobel. He invented dynamite. It was a wonderful tool for industry. It saved a lot of lives by keeping people from having to use the more dangerous explosive nitro-glycerin. Now, a lot of people got killed from dynamite. But it made the money for the Nobel Prizes. So, inventions aren't always bad or good, but can have intentions of each. It depends on the intentions of the inventor and the designs of those that employ it."

"Nobel Prize," Ted started in on his retort, and then got distracted. "Hey, there are napkins in here. Do you realize how long it has been since I've had a napkin? I didn't realize it until just now. Even when you gave me one it didn't sink in. I usually wipe my face with used newspaper, not to mention other things I wipe with them. But back to Alfie, that's what I call Alfred Nobel. Well, well, we should wonder why old Alfie started this benevolent prize thing. My dad used to call this kind of thing fire insurance. It was fire insurance because people like Alfie thought that by showing charity to people they could save themselves from the flames of hell. They rationalize their reprehensible behavior in life, by believing being charitable mitigates all of the horrors they have perpetrated on humanity." He paused and laughed. "Am I part of your own fire insurance?"

"You are not my fire insurance. Charity is a way to settle my spirit. I haven't done anything in my life to fear hell. You, on the other hand, have something to fear. As long as we are referencing religious principles, you should reflect on one biblical story. A man gave two of his servants ten talents each. A talent was a measure of money in those days. One of the servants went and made more money with his talents, the other servant buried the talents he was given. The one who made more money with his talents was praised. The one who did nothing with his talents was cursed and damned. Do you understand?"

With the last bit of food on the table stuffed in his face Ted commented, "Wasn't Jesus broke? I mean, he told the rich man to give away all his possessions to find salvation. I guess I beat the moral on that story by not having any talents monetarily or mentally. You can't damn me or curse me for that. Anyway, I can't imagine a good and loving God damning me to hell for eternity for being a lazy nitwit. I believe people with brains and talents are more likely to fry in the eternal lake of fire like a pig on a spit than people with no possessions like me. I've got nothing, dude, and to me that must mean I've got salvation. That thought keeps me happy in the worst of times. Now, all of religion might be a sack of crap, but you have to have a mental wheel chair when you are a mental paraplegic. Marx said that religion was the opiate of the people. I think that religion is more a coping device for living. Whether there is a God or not if the idea of religion helps people deal with the problems of their day to day living, then I'm all for it. Me? I don't need religion to cope. I cope by getting real drunk and stupid. After all, ignorance is bliss." Ted then, for effect, drained his glass of wine.

"Religion helps sometimes," said William. "Maybe you have no reason to be religious. But I need something to keep me upright and breathing. Maybe you are the reincarnation of Nostradamus or a male version of the Oracle of Delphi. I'm feeling a little exposed by you. You've nailed every tragedy in my life. My wife has left me and I've lost my job. I can't lose my religion. I wouldn't know where to go or what to do without my faith. I thought I was a good husband. I thought I was a good employee." He put his head back on the table and crossed his arms around the front of his head on the table.

Ted leaned forward to pat the disheveled man on the shoulder again. "Dude, the magnificence of idiocy is having no worries. Your wife probably had reasons to leave you and your boss probably had reasons to fire you. But who cares? I had a friend when I was younger who used to say, 'Don't know, don't care, and don't give a damn'. This is my religion for life and it makes me happy. You can't change history. What *was* was, period. It's important to remember some things, but more important to forget others. I swear, I can't even remember my ex-wife's name and I sure can't figure out where I used to work. Ease is the only romance I want these days and to live each moment like it was my last; Carpe diem dude."

"Carpe diem," mumbled the crumpled hulk on the table. "How do you forget? How do you forget the horrors of life? How do you take in each breath knowing that when you exhale your problems will still be there?"

"Mr. Wanky Duck," Ted responded without hesitation.

"What?" asked William with the word 'what' dripping with incredulity. He then lifted his head from the table.

"Mr. Wanky Duck swims in the lake every day. He's my favorite duck, well; maybe Mr. Wanky Duck is a she. Then I would have to call it Mrs. Wanky Duck. Hmm, if she was single, I guess I would then have to call her Miss Wanky Duck. But if I was around some progressive feminist I would have to call her Ms. Wanky Duck. I guess that's why I stick to Mr. Wanky Duck. It's safer that way."

William leaned back, groaned and slid low in the bench seat. "Is there a point to this? What does Mr., Miss, Mrs., or Ms., Wanky duck have to do with what I'm going through?" He wrapped his arms over his head and slid a little lower.

"Well Billy, I feed Mr. Wanky Duck almost every day. I bring him some crumbs left over from whatever I scavenged from the dumpster. I've fed Mr. Wanky Duck several hundred times at least. But he still doesn't recognize me. I have to follow him down the grass walk way watching him waddle. It's only when he sees the crumbs does he stop and start eating. He never remembers me, but he doesn't forget how to eat. There are two ways I could handle my feelings for Mr. Wanky Duck. One way would to have me get resentful of him not showing gratitude for my benevolence. The second way is to find satisfaction that I did something nice for a really dumb creature and not worry about the response. I know that Mr. Wanky Duck is happier with a full belly than an empty one. But Mr. Wanky Duck can never tell me that. I can take pleasure in watching him waddle on the grass or paddle in the water. But if I want pleasure by getting his attention and wanting gratitude, I would be sorely disappointed by his behavior. I choose the waddle and paddling and it works for our relationship. But I have no illusions that Mr. Wanky Duck will at sometime go away forever."

The frumpy waitress brought out the cherry pie and had it a la mode with a blob of vanilla ice cream. She plopped the saucer on the table, collected the used dishes and said, "There's no charge for the ice cream. Anyone who talks to ducks needs a treat." She then went back behind her fortress of solitude: the counter,

William watched Ted devour the cherry pie while thinking about what Ted had said. William was wondering if any of the things Ted had said were worthy of merit. "I suppose," he started, lowering his arms and sitting up straight, "that I get a bit of your metaphor. You should only care about a person as much as they care about you. Is that it?"

"Hmph," grunted Ted shaking his head back and forth, mouth full of cherry pie; He swallowed hard and said, "No."

"No?"

"I wanted to convey the idea that it doesn't matter what the other person does. You only need to be proud of what you do. If their response isn't what you like, you should realize that maybe that's all they are capable of giving. Mr. Wanky Duck isn't exhibiting things like vindictiveness he just isn't capable of showing affection. Maybe your wife was incapable of appreciating the things you did for her. Maybe your boss was too overcome by his own responsibilities to be able to recognize a good employee. Neither one these situations is a reflection on you. Hell, Mr. Wanky Duck's inattention to me doesn't make me feel inadequate. The lessons I learned interacting with him actually helped me to a more enlightened state. What's bad about that?"

"There's nothing wrong with seeking enlightenment," said William, exiting a groan again, "but you should probably seek enlightenment from someone other than a duck. I mean, you've quoted some incredible philosophers. You should even read the quotes of Samuel Clemmons, or some lowlife like Hunter S. Thompson, but not a damn duck. There are many, many people who have said profound things that you can reflect upon."

"Did the ideas and writing of these people help keep you from sitting on a curb in a fifteen hundred dollar suit sulking and crying? I used to sit on the curb and sob about my existence. But, since I met Mr. Wanky Duck I haven't had to sit on any curb. I always figure that I'm not smart enough to really understand what renowned philosophers say, even though I have a minor in philosophy. I guess that's why I know that most philosophers are full of crap. Hell, after thou and thus in the first sentence of the text, I didn't know what they meant. But I can understand a duck. You shouldn't be so arrogant that you think that you can outthink a duck. They know how to eat, poop and procreate. What else is there beyond that?"

"Ted," whispered William, while leaning forward over the table, "there is love. Humans need love and you can't deny that." His hand quivered with emphasis. "Love has been taken away from me. When I was in love, I was in heaven. Now I'm in hell."

Knitting up his brow, Ted started, "A couple points of order," he said, "first of all, how do we know if a duck doesn't need love? Humans can ascribe emotions to many animals for needing attention and affection by how they act as an instance of love, especially dogs. I had a dog once and I loved her. I liked to think that she loved me. Maybe she did, maybe she didn't. I will never actually know. We can't be a dog or a duck, so we don't know how the calculus of love comes into play in their existence.

"Anymore, all I care about now is loving others and myself. If it turns out that someone or something loves me back then it is a bonus. But getting love shouldn't be an ultimatum for having a relationship with anything. If you love the beauty of a tree, it's not going to give you a hug. If you have to demand love from someone or something, then the relationship is not worth having. And, by the way, it is my personal belief that the idea of heaven is overrated. Think about it. How long will avenues of gold remain valuable to you? How long will your mansion be of wonderment? And, how long will it be a pleasure to sing songs at the right hand of God? To hell with that garbage, for me heaven is on earth in the form of a duck, tree and a second hand hamburger."

"Ted," said William, slumping back into his green, cracked vinyl bench seat, "if heaven is on earth, why does it feel like hell? And how will I get to this heaven?" The last sentence was spit out with a tinge of vehemence.

"I heard a story about the concept of heaven once," Ted said, then took a swig of beer and swished it around in his mouth before swallowing. "As the story goes, there are a bunch of little worms in the bottom of a swamp."

"What?" yelled William, more agitated than he had been before.

Holding both of his hands up, as if to say 'stop', and rolling his eyes Ted said, "You need to let me finish. So, there are these worms in the swamp. Every once in a while one of them felt the need to climb up the stem of a lily pad. Once one of them did, they would never come back. Well, a group of worm buddies made a pact. If one of them felt the compunction to go up the stem, then they would promise to come back and tell them what it was like up above. Well, one of the worms got the urge to go up and it did go up. When it got to the top of the lily pad, it crawled out on the large flat leaf and was blinded by the sun. The little worm fell asleep on the warm lily pad and wondered why he hadn't already gone back down to his friends. When it woke from the slumber, it had many new feelings. The drowsiness went away and he rose above the lily pad with wonderment. The little worm had become a butterfly and flew around for a while. He then remembered the friends down in the swamp. The new butterfly came close to the surface of the water and could see its friends on the bottom and it knew they could see this flapping creature as it had seen such things from the bottom of the swamp. He wanted to explain to them what had happened, but they couldn't hear or recognize the former friend."

"Oh damn," said William, slumping once again down into his ratty bench seat, "what the hell does that have to do with me? I've already climbed up a lily pad stem to get to heaven and ended up in hell. That's where I am now. I want to know how to get to heaven."

"When I quit my job, whatever it was," Ted started, "people thought I was crazy and lazy. When I divorced my wife, whoever she was, people ridiculed me for giving up on a hopeless relationship. When I gave what's her name everything rather than go through the humiliation of divorce court people thought I had given up on life. From their side of the swamp, from the muck of the mud, they couldn't recognize that I had metamorphosed into a different and better being. Everyone saw my behavior as incomprehensible and incompetent. But they couldn't realize that I was entering my particular heaven which made me not recognizable and not comprehensible from their muddy bottom of the swamp of their life. Maybe, just maybe, you are exiting your swamp and into your heaven. Don't let people's misunderstanding keep you from flying."

After another big sigh, William said, "I guess I get your point. I was miserable in marriage and I was miserable at work. I have to decide what it was that I lost and what I gained. I feel sometimes like I'm pressed between two realities that are trying to squeeze something out of me like olives in a press. Please tell me that there is living to all of this. Tell me there are goals of determinant nature which are worth living for."

"Sure," said Ted, "the answer is doing what you want to do. If you do that, then you are living life. As long as you walk down the path of life you want, happiness will follow."

Shaking his head up and down William said, "Okay, okay, I need to go now and get some things done. I'll pay the bill. Have a good day. Thanks for the conversation. I'd like to talk to you again sometime."

"Well, I think you have the rough vicinity of where my box is. I don't plan on going anywhere soon, though moving wouldn't be difficult."

As William pulled himself out of the booth and stood, Ted asked, "Are you going to take that bagel?"

An Answer to a Question

He pulled the wire rimmed glasses off his face to wipe them with his yellowing handkerchief, replaced them, and then peered at me again as if it were his first inspection. "An interesting question," he said in his raspy grandfatherly tone, "and one which carries with it a broad spectrum of baggage. I hope I can, for you, remain concise." The gaze became less focused and drifted right through me to become lost in thought. After some time I began to think he had lost interest.

"Would you like me to come back," I say peering into his face for some sign of cognition, "after you've had some time to think about it?" The pressure for a response seemed to make him nervous.

He heaved himself out of his squeaky office chair and began to fidget about the cluttered office by pulling and poking at stacks of paper and books or trying to arrange his over long curly white fringe of hair with exaggerated strokes of the hand. He came upon an old small dusty globe sitting on a shelf without a stand. Picking it up with one large hand he unexpectedly spit on it then used the sleeve of his droopy gray sweater to wipe it clean. Mumbling through an index finger pressed to his lips he said, "It looked a lot different then. Yes, yes, it was a lot different then." He pulled the globe close squashing up his entire face to meet the squinting demand of his eyes. "We had two less states then and about half the people... so many people these days... coming from everywhere. I suppose it just reflects the population growth in the rest of the world... much less in some cases. Yet, still, there are so many people. Here." He offers me the globe on an outstretched palm. "Have you ever seen one this old?"

I looked it over noticing that Germany was shown as including Austria and the Sudetenland. This put its age at around 1940. "Yes," I replied feeling quite scholarly at determining the age, "I do believe I've seen several from this era." The big hand twisted the globe in mine until East Africa and most of Southern Asia was visible.

"Look at that would you?" he said easing his backside onto the edge of the desk with a low groan. "Great Britain still owned half the world then. You're probably too young to have heard this but they used to say 'The sun never sets on the British Empire'."

"Yes I've heard..."

"It was physically quite true at the time," he went on, irking me by not being interested in my response. "As you go around this globe, you see here, there is somewhere where there are daylight hours on a British colony. Now, I suppose they also wanted you to be interested in the figurative sense of the phrase. But it was the literal sense of it which intrigued me as a young man." He leaned back his head to let his bifocals do more of the work in seeing the detail, letting his mouth droop open as if the mechanics of the two were related. "Yes, this old globe tells quite a story." After another long pause, he enraptured with inspecting the small orb, I started again.

"Yes, that's fine Dr. Menlo. But now back to my..."

"Oh, look at this," he said, interrupting me again. "Tibet is still an independent country. It's been so long it causes one to forget it was the case at one time. It is a shame that the communists are so recalcitrant. I think it is a culture that the world could learn a lot from. It really is a shame that such a kind and loving people could be trod under the hobnail boots of domination." The yellowing handkerchief came out of the back pocket again this time to dabble unnecessarily at his forehead and sagging jowls. He shoved the rag back into his pocket looking up from the globe to make eye contact with me. Noticing my impatient expression he continued, "Ah, yes, yes, to your question. You have to forgive the older folk we're not as empathetic as we should be to the petulance of youth. I was quite petulant as a young man." He paused while scratching at his freckled bald head. "Hmmm, is that the word I'm looking for? Perhaps I'm getting that mixed up with corpulent. It is a shame to grow older, you know. The vocabulary I spent a lifetime building to express myself is turning into a ball of mush." On the corner of his desk was a thick, well thumbed dictionary, which he leaned over to pick up. "This is the only book in here that I consistently know the whereabouts of," he continued. "Probably the only book that I really... should... ah, here we are, corpulence; a noun meaning fatness. Ha! That's why I got them mixed up. I used to be petulant and now I'm corpulent." He patted the front of his white shirt stretched taut by the expanded belly behind, all the while inspecting the dictionary as if some other definition of the word were lurking between the lines. "Hmmm, yes, corpulent and petulant...words which sound so much a like... but so different." He set down the dictionary in its well known position with a heaving sigh. He glanced first at me, then to all corners of the room then to the floor, his head hanging low.

"This is for Dr...uh... Dr....Dr. Howard's class," the old man said. "Yes, yes, Dr. Howard's class. He does this type of thing too me quite often. I've then thought about this type of question quite often." The old professor leaned back on the desk looking toward the ceiling with his arms folded about his middle. He alternately puckered and stretched tight his lips as if his mouth were a pump trying to prime fuel to his brain. With two smacks of his dry lips, he began again. "I saw the moon last night. It poked its pretty little head out from behind the fog for just a few moments. It's one thing I don't enjoy very much about the fall here, the fog. It's not so bad if you don't have to drive... kind of spooky at times... all in all not pleasant. It was bright, this moon, unusually clear coming through the fog. You don't often get that clear view of the moon coming through the fog. It is about a half moon these days and I wasn't sure, just by looking at it, whether the thing was waxing or waning. I suppose if I were an astronomer, or even perhaps slightly competent in those sorts of things, I would probably be... uh... yes, able to tell. You're getting the point, I assume?"

The question was asked without eye contact as he was busy wiping his glasses one more time. I was about to reply that his ambiguous point was well understood when he went on to tell me the answer to his own question. "The obvious point to the story is being that we don't often know that things happening slowly are happening at all, let alone know the direction of events. This particular event, the moon going through its phases, is interesting as an analogy for many reasons." He stopped to glare at my little tape recorder. The brow knitted suddenly seeming distressed; as if it were the first time he was aware of it. "You're supposed to interview and critique my response?" he asked, still glaring at the little machine.

"Well, you or someone else," I replied, setting the recorder on his desk beside him for more obvious inspection. He picked it up and rotated it this way and that finally replacing it on the desk to wipe his hand free of its influence on his sweater.

"Damn little things," he said wheezing out a snicker, "I'm sure I don't sound like that big a blithering idiot while I'm saying what I say. Those little stinkers can make me sound down right stupid later though." He gave me an abbreviated smile. I shrugged my shoulders. He pushed himself off the desk with another groan and began again fidgeting around the room. "Yes," he said softly, "I suppose you're interested in the answer... hmmmm... ha... the answer." As one big, gnarled hand drug across a row of books it stopped suddenly and flicked out a volume with surprising dexterity and speed. "Here we are," he said smiling back at me as if the answer had just been found. "Roman Art, what a fascinating book. You know, these Romans weren't nearly as dull or insensitive to form or content as we like to believe. I think a lot of that comes from our Judeo-Christian outlook on things. Both the Jews and Christians largely vilify the Romans. Not without foundation, mind you... throwing someone to lions isn't a way to endear you to someone." He began flipping through the pages breathing shallow sharp breaths lost in thought.

I became very impatient and began looking around the room myself. My study partner, James, had warned me about interviewing Dr. Menlo. "That old dusty fart?" he had sneered incredulously, "I don't care what Dr. Howard says, Dr. Menlo is so out of it he wouldn't know he was on fire if a smoke alarm went off." I began to imagine this silly old man's body starting to smoke furiously while sitting in his office chair, droning on without a clue, and finally bursting into a ball of flame. I think a smile even crept across my face when a book snapping shut suddenly caught my attention. Dr. Menlo was staring at me over the top of his glasses. In the way he looked at me, it seemed as if he somehow knew what I was thinking. It made me feel uncomfortable and I slid around in the soft vinyl chair to avoid his gaze.

"These Romans weren't dull people," he went on "They spent a lot of time thinking about their lot in life. They didn't have all the distractions that we do, such as T.V. and radio and all. I'm pretty sure a lot of them were aware of the fact that they were in trouble towards the end. A lot of them realized the nobility was slipping a cog or two. But they didn't really know why. People like Nero or Caligula were crazy as a hoot and people knew it. But when you're emperor there aren't a lot of people you listen to, especially if you're crazy. And there weren't a lot of people who were willing to criticize a man who could have you tortured to death.

"Lead lined pots of wine were what it was. The rich nobility could afford to have their wine preserved in these fancy lead lined pots. A sort of keeping up with the Caesar's kind of thing and everybody who was somebody had these damned lead lined pots. It was thought of as a preservative of sorts. Well you and I know that lead isn't good for you and it's much worse for your offspring. The sons and daughters of these rich people came out dull and irritable. I guess it isn't easy to run an empire when you're dull and irritable, hence, the empire declined and eventually fell... end of story." He pulled open the book and snapped it shut again for dramatic effect.

"And so it's your opinion," I ventured, "that we are in decline, like the Romans." His mouth pump began priming his brain again, this time faster, and with his brow knit up signifying either disappointment or confusion. "Or... uhm... maybe I'm misunderstanding your point."

His primer suddenly stopped, easing in to what could be described as a subtle grin. He walked around to the other side of the old fashioned dark oak desk and, with both hands, eased himself slowly into the weathered office chair with another long groan. The streaks of ghostly fall sun light coming through the sanctuary like window intensified the silence of the room. The creaking of the chair as he leaned back to cross his legs seemed amplified in the tomb like silence of the room. Everything in the room suddenly seemed a preparation for the solemnity of a casket; a pseudo-sarcophagus where even the beating of someone's heart could be heard as a disturbance.

When the silence became enough for me to scream, he gave me a reply. "Understanding or misunderstanding a point isn't appropriate at this juncture since I haven't finished making it yet, there will be plenty of time for misunderstanding it later." He looked at me to laugh, but turned toward the window to continue, probably noticing my indignant expression. "Whoever was the joker who invented the lead lined pot thought he was doing his bosses a favor. A lot of things you read about in history are like that. Things that seem an improvement to people at the time... later seen as... uh... not so well.

"I was just finishing my college career when DDT came on the market with some fanfare. At the time it was a miracle substance. People thought we would now forever be free of unwanted little pests. If you've ever spent any time in the South, where I was going to school you know the problem with ticks and fleas that they have. Well, this was going to rid your backyard of these disease carrying parasites. Spritz one little can of this goop on your lawn and then you could roll around on the green grass of home without fear of collecting fleas, ticks and chiggers faster than your dog. We actually thought the world would be free of all disease carrying parasites... mosquitoes and the like. We would free the world of malaria, bubonic plague, and a host of other things. Some very noble thinking went into stinking up the whole planet with this stuff. We realized, much too late of course, that all these pests became immune to DDT. We weren't just killing pests and that it wasn't all that good for you or I.

"There are plenty of other examples. This is just one that comes to mind. People really believed this stuff greatly improved their quality of life and in a microcosm of the times they were right." He clasped his weathered hands behind him and turned to me, "You are a... a..." he said blinking as he stammered in his in-determinant question. "What would you be? A... a... well, with Doctor Howard you must be a Soph... No, at least a junior taking American History."

"A Senior," I replied pointing to my class ring.

"Oh yes, not one of those juniors." Dr. Menlo came back with a strange amount of emphasis on the word Junior. "You've ascended the ranks now and are in charge of the Senior Square and the mascot and all other such symbols due the journeymen of our fair school." He paused to peer at me with his eyebrows raised high, his mouth bent in a patronizing frog like leer, waiting for a response.

"Yes I am. I mean, yes I have."

"You do consider this an improvement for you on this campus, don't you?"

"Yes, quite."

"Yes, quite," he repeated giggling to himself over some inner joke. "Yes, I suppose it is quite an improvement." He stood and walked to the front of the desk again and heaved himself onto one corner with a sigh, the head cocking again towards the ceiling with the mouth agape. "When I was a senior here I thought it was quite an improvement myself. I was, believe it or not, captain of the football team. I was a decent athlete, though not an exceptional one. Yet at the time I was.... well... hmmmm.... had a high opinion of my own ability. I was a very capable student in academics. Yet, I sincerely believed my real talent lie on the field, thereby finding a happy rational for avoiding my studies. Yes, I thought I was quite the athlete." He stood up, tucked a mock football under his arm, and crouched staring toward the opposite wall as if it were an opponent. "Yes, I was infamous for a rather vicious straight arm while running. Those were the days of the leather helmets; the ones without face masks. So a vicious straight arm was a... well... more, uh... a potent deterrent to being tackled. Yes, I was quite a player when compared with the players of other small private schools. I was sure that my prominent position as a player in our league would easily translate into a wonderful scholarship to the State University. Well, my braggadocio never panned out, and the scholarship never came. I probably could have received an academic scholarship, but my fatuous state had let my grades slip dismally. At the time I was never happier. I thought I had really reached the pinnacle of High School success. But it... hmmm... didn't really... uh... end up that way." He hung his head wiping his glasses one more time as if the shame of failure was still fresh in his mind.

"It put my education back a few years," he went on, replacing his handkerchief and glasses. "I couldn't afford to go straight away to college, so I went to work on the farm. I did a lot of growing up and ate a lot of crow on that farm. The other workers, all older, liked to point out my shortcomings and rub them in my face. To them I was too slow, too stupid, too pious and too young to be of any good to anybody. I didn't enjoy those two years. They were... uh... could have been... uh..."

"Excuse me Dr. Menlo," I broke in while looking at my watch, "perhaps we could get back to the analogy of the moon phases."

He peered forward at me as if confused, then pulled the glasses off rubbing his entire face up and down with a sound of dry rustling leaves. The glasses went back on; both hands guiding the ear pieces carefully into place. His big hands slapped softly onto his knees as he stood one more time with a heaving sigh. "Yes," he said giving me an irritated glance, "I did promise to try and be concise." He stood stretching out the loose skin under his neck staring toward the wall. The deathly silence had fallen again, this time for an unbearable length of time. He stood with his mouth gaping open as if mesmerized by the textured plaster of the wall he was staring at. His breathing became so shallow and regular I almost believed he had fallen asleep on his feet.

The words of my study partner came back to haunt me one more time. "Maybe I should set the old fart on fire," I thought to myself. "He would surely be a little livelier that way; my god, why did I take Dr. Howard's advice and interview this geriatric old dork?" I began shaking my leg up and down on the ball of my foot with impatience. I looked at my watch again and began thinking of excuses to leave when, without looking away from his hypnotic spot, he started again.

"What do you think... uh... about this project... well, the question? Yes, the question itself, what do you think about the question?"

I was so thankful to have the silence broken that I responded forgetting to be annoyed that it was I who was supposed to be interviewing him. "Not much of a question for a history class I suppose," I opined crossing my arms in front of me. "The whole thing seems more of an exercise for Dr. Howard's curiosity rather than in... well... in ...

"In the study of History?" Dr. Menlo offered finally turning away from his focused position toward me.

"Why, yes, I guess what I'm trying to say is that I don't realize the purpose of the exercise. It's also kind of ambiguous. Like the last part of it, 'what is your opinion and the opinion of a member of the faculty'? I guess I really don't see the question as a matter of opinion. Like History, I think a state of being is much more a matter of fact than a matter of opinion."

Dr. Menlo's eyes focused in on me with a disturbing amount of intensity. He slapped his hands behind his back and began tapping one foot. "Ah, yes, history as a matter of fact," he started with an air of sarcasm. "Such as: the year Columbus sailed the ocean blue or the number of casualties in the first hour in the battle of Coal Harbor or the names of all the Presidents. In that way, Historians aren't much more than bean counters." He finished off the sentence with a snort and walked slowly around the back of me continuing his laser like stare. I had apparently resurrected a long buried pet peeve of his and it made me feel uncomfortable to bare the brunt of its ire. He finished his full circle around to sit back on the same corner of the desk. "And what are the facts concerning your state of being right now?" he asked with the intonation of a teacher, less irritated, yet still instructional.

"I suppose I feel pretty good."

"Do you suppose or is it true?"

"Yes, it's true. I feel pretty good."

"And what do you suppose is my opinion on your state of being?"

I suddenly became defensive. He was ignoring my question and badgering me with this inane line of questioning. After pausing to think, I came back less defensively than I wanted to, "I don't really care what your opinion on that is. That is, I don't think it matters."

"And," he continued unperturbed by my response, "how should the fact that you don't care about my opinion influence what I think about your state of being? And what if I'm wondering about your state of being today, years from now, perhaps, long after you are gone?" He let the question sit in silence for a while then rose to stare out the steeple window. His form loomed large in the soft light. "Historians are only men," he said straightening, "trying to unravel the mysteries of reality with the benefit of hindsight. You should realize that this project is less for the curiosity of Dr. Howard than it will be, years hence, for your own. It will be then when you will fully realize the worth of your 'facts' on our state of being at the present." The erect old professor now spun to look at me with his hands on his hips. He looked stern and fatherly; the origin of either of these expressions was lost on me. I felt as if he were venting on me some old grudge never fully reconciled. I was absorbing the shock from a diatribe originally designed to blow off steam at someone who had riled the old buzzard years ago. His beady eyes glowered at me. I crossed my legs and slid low on the slippery vinyl covering, my arms lashed around my middle. The silence, which before had been dreary and solemn, was now charged with electricity, leaving me to again search for an uneasy exit from the office. I sat staring at the back of the desk then glanced at my watch. When I glanced up at Dr. Menlo his gaze had softened considerably.

With a heaving sigh his hands fell back to his side and the shoulders drooped to their normal position. "The point of all... uh... this being," he said wringing his dry hands, "is, of course, that... well... reality isn't all that easy to perceive... uhm... as easy as it seems to perceive correctly." The musty rag came out of the back pocket to get patted around the back of his neck. He swallowed hard pressing his lips together firmly then eased into the high backed chair which groaned his arrival. "I... uh... like you," he went on softly, creaking his seat into lounge position, "believe this exercise is pointless... er... not pointless but... uh ... extraneous, yes, extraneous. Yet, I think so for many different reasons.

"For me, it's extraneous since I've spent years trying to do it and, for that reason, perhaps, I see its futility. You, on the other hand, don't yet see... well... grasp... uhm... It's something you need to do, like swallowing a bitter pill, but shouldn't ... well... This isn't coming out very well at all." Both hands went on top of his head and began kneading the hairless scalp like an over stiff lump of dough. He rubbed back and forth while staring at the ceiling as if he were trying to squeeze the thoughts from his brain into his mouth. The chair creaked forward and the hands came off the head to smack down in a matter of fact fashion on the desk to signify an idea really had oozed out of his mind into his mouth.

"You mentioned getting back to the analogy of the moon. I think that would be helpful at this time." The chair eased back into the lounge position giving him the opportunity to strike a thoughtful pose; elbows on each arm of the chair with the digits of each hand meeting at the tips. "Let us suppose we realize, after careful study, we know the moon is waning. We spent all night one night studying the moon with careful measuring devices and now we know the silly thing is getting smaller and will continue to do so. Now, does knowing that fact influence how the moon behaves? No, of course not, the moon will continue to grow less prominent each night and not give a hoot as to our learned methodology. In a week or two, every man on the street will be aware of the fact. Even the dullest Joe Blow will be able to determine the direction, eventually, with or without our conclusions. Perhaps, if we were very fast, we could issue a detailed report for one and all to read presenting our results on the state of the moon before every man on the street were aware of it. Thereby collect accolades for our scholarly prediction as to the inevitable. Unless, of course, we were in such a hurry to outrun the inevitable that we miscalculated our prediction and concluded that the thing was actually waxing. That would be, well... uh... humorous, but not at all uncommon in this day and age. Well, anyway, the moon won't change if we know it is waning, and even if we are very curious we won't know that much further in advance than the average Joe, so, well... uh... There you have it." He slapped his hands onto the arms of the chair giving me a tight lipped satisfied look.

"Well then," I ventured, "it is then your opinion that our nation is loosing influence as a world power and that this decline is inevitable like the phases of the moon." At this point the old professor's mouth dropped open, as if from great fatigue, and he emitted a most peculiar groan which finished off at the end with a barely audible "Oh, nuts."

"Hmmm...Well... yes...," he started, pulling off his glasses and again rasping one hand up and down across his face. He was sounding suddenly older and more tired, speaking in abbreviated gasps, not stirring from his lounge position. "I did promise to be concise. The point I'm trying to make though not, I must confess, in the most efficacious manner is that the question has a myriad of solutions. A 'yes we are' or 'no we aren't' are both at once correct. We could take the map of Germany on that small globe and analyze its world influence and whether or not this improved the lives of its inhabitants. You could rightly argue in either direction. It surely was increasing as a world power and many people were much better off. Yet, at the same time, a cancer was eating away at its very fabric and it was positioning itself on a precipice of total destruction. Good or bad, yes or no simply do not apply them to the question at hand. Any analysis of the short term is frivolous. Which leaves analysis in the long term which is akin to having a crystal ball and one might as well toss a coin.

"So, as brief as... well... an old duffer can be. Shakespeare said brevity is the sole of wit, so I can't believe I'm very witty. But to put it as plain as possible... well... uh... ha, ha... maybe, not plain but blunt. The careful study of History, the study of, reality, if you will, even with the benefit of 20/20 hindsight, doesn't always draw a clear picture. Therefore, to predict the course of events on the present, let alone the future, on such a grand scale would be nothing less than the highest form of intellectual pomposity. Though, there are whole crews of men and women who make large sums of money doing just such things. People like Economists or these think tank wizards. Think tank, ha, now there's a contradiction in... Uh... well, if not terms then in practice... more like a dogma tank. Anyway, predicting anymore than the most obvious event is not worth the time of analysis. Though, through the study of History, it is very important to be able to predict these obvious events. Such as we have seen in the failure and cruelty of Fascism, or what recent events have shown to be the failure of centrally planned economies. Now, to even these obvious conclusions men will turn a blind eye when they so desire. It is difficult, if not impossible, to underestimate the ability of men to blind themselves to the obvious. So, you can begin your report not with a definitive yes or no, from me, but with a... ha, ha... very fuzzy maybe."

By this time the old professor's voice had become a buzz-like drone bouncing off the walls and my ears. He was staring off toward the ceiling looking both pleased and enraptured with his gabbling. My mood had become dreary enough to no longer even be haunted with the words of my study partner. It was in this dreary state of quasi-somnambulism that I let a long yawn slip. When I had finished blinking my teary eyes I noticed that Dr. Menlo had again focused his gaze on me. It wasn't the laser guided stare of before. Maybe the sharpness of focus of that stare was lost in what was now in his fog. This gaze was more quizzical, a questioning gaze that cast an uncertain air about an otherwise flat affect.

"Perhaps it should be mentioned," he said slowly raising his bushy eyebrows, "that no exercise is totally futile if it requires you to seek the opinions of others. We as a society have become very wrapped up in our own individual opinions. This leads to people taking themselves entirely too serious. It makes people insufferably fatuous. It is also... uh... well, good that Dr. Howard is making you take advantage of those of us who have seen... hmmm... by nature of just having been around so long. When you've been around long enough any dunderhead can, by mere weight of years and experience, be a valuable resource for one thing or another. So it's... uh... I think... uh... good, better than...well... uh... Is there any question that you have to continue the discussion?"

"No," I said immediately seizing the opportunity to leave. I stood up, picked up my tape recorder, and glanced at my watch for effect. "No, I think that will suffice. Thank you very much for your time Dr. Menlo." The old professor's face sagged a bit at my hurry to get away.

"Well then," he said politely while standing to see me out, "let me know how it goes. And if you have anything else you would like to discuss I would be glad to help."

With a perfunctory "thank you" I slipped out the door into the high ceiling tiled hallway. The clicking of hard soled shoes echoing down the corridor sounded deliciously lively as compared to the sarcophagus I had just left. One set of heels belonged to my study partner James. He walked right up to me with a smirk on his face, jabbing me with his index finger in the chest.

"I can tell by the look on your face," He said, "I told you the old buzzard would drive you out of your mind.

"Yeah," I responded, "I don't know why I bothered."

Shadow Dancing: A Spiritual Twist

Light shone splendidly through the cherry blossoms, warming my skin and alleviating the subtle aches and pains I carry with me stoically from day to day. Reaching up to one of the small, spindly branches that splayed out from the young arbor I pulled it close to drink in the fragrance. Spring, I thought, such a magnificent time of release from the grips of winter and a time when one could think of love. Perhaps that was it; I think now. Perhaps it was my preoccupation with thoughts of love that led me to such a state of chagrin. Or maybe it was the realization that the blossoms were plum and not cherry. In either case the die was cast and I set out on a most peculiar course.

Along the sidewalk the humble, small trees stood as testament to the ability to survive the ice of life, sprouting from small patches of earth left between the sidewalk and asphalt of the main road of our simple town. I walked for pleasure's sake; sake I consider most pleasing. And as I walked those thoughts of spring sprang into my mind. The air was fresh and I was on my way to get a daily chronicle to remind myself of the hopeless muck that most of the world is mired in and, by contrast, help myself to an advancing mood. Coffee, as always, would accompany my journey further piquing my air of interest in the pleasures at hand. Ahead of me, most innocuous, walked a thin, nicely shaped woman, younger than I, yet not so young as one might put notions of such a coupling well beyond reason. The full, plump buttocks loped from side to side, alone on the sidewalk, inside the tight accouterments out of sight of a wondering eye. Thinking to myself I suppose I was musing of such a coupling when I thought again how strange it might seem to such a young and pretty girl, staidly dressed, plain hair and knit cap that I should be staring at her on such a lonely street. The thought that I thought, the second not the first, mixed into me while I noticed the shapely posterior until I noticed that the head of the ensemble had turned and was noticing me notice the rest. Our eyes met, and to my horror, her glance was fearful. I do admit I must have drawn out of my mixing feelings an expression akin to guilt, perhaps influencing a reaction in her mind. A mind certainly made wary of day to day living and the motives of men by such muck as emanates from a daily chronicle that I was about to purchase. Such muck came to my mind, having read it day to day, and it spurred my remorse. She spun back to her forward proximity and increased in haste.

All embarrassment followed. I, after all, am not one to deny himself a gratuitous peek from time to time. In fact, I find the perusing of the female form a sort of diversion of mine that I am not the least bit ashamed of. Yet, alone on that street, having my mood misread, I found myself in a bit of a pinch. I felt almost like crossing the street, or turning the other way in order to cancel the possibility of further misunderstanding. Retreat, though consulted, was not in my plans. Chalking it up to some cruel probability of timing, I realized that the encounter was probably only one of those crazy little things one bears from time to time along the rocky highway of life. I continued my brisk walk.

Difficult as it was trying not to notice the fanciful curves as I walked along, I had to in order to suspend the potentiality of further interaction. I had no intent of harassment or bringing an atmosphere even close to it. Yet, it wasn't to be. Perhaps the sweet spring air caused me to take the situation lightly. As I found myself reminiscing about the misdiagnosis of her urban paranoia, in a move nearly reflexive, before I could gain muscle control over my orbs, I glanced to her anew. And as calamity would have it, she looked back again at that very instant catching me with a nervous smile.

This time I was flummoxed. I found myself fumbling nervously to place my swinging arms into my pockets. I coughed a silly cough and looked to the sidewalk. I did not dare feign an examination, but

I am sure that she must have glanced at me one more time. Evidence for this presupposition comes from the fact that she suddenly changed course; this presumed since I did not change mine and supposed that she intended to change hers to be rid of me or find my proper intentions. Store fronts along the street all have a recessed vestibule between their front windows accommodating the main entrance. My fair lady suddenly scooted into one such recess and pretended to look for something in her handbag as I walked by.

How, you might think, did I know what she was doing if I was not looking? It was a wary and subtle eye I was casting at that point, low to the ground beneath her feet or wide to one side relying slyly on the peripheral vision--and I do have excellent peripheral vision. Anyhow, I thought the situation guardedly passed and I continued down the pretty spring lane.

Along the road, as one reaches the larger part of downtown, there are stop lights, some rather lengthy. I fully intended to cross the street, moving straight to the paper vending machines. The fine young lady, however, caught my attention again. The light, crossing the road, had just turned red and the sign held up that red electronic hand only mistakable as the symbol to stop by un-bred macaques. As I tarried for the green marker that would allow my peripatetic morning to continue I heard her footsteps coming up to one side. You can only imagine my angst.

Off my right shoulder I could feel her lurking there, her presence penetrating my psychic space as surely as a submarine violates a sonar beacon. I could sense her inquiring presence probing my motives yet I dare not look. Twice before I had played the fool sneaking such glances and I could not suffer another such debacle. Like a dying man who knows that the vulture of death is perched on his shoulder but cannot admit it, I could not stare into the eyes of something so forbidden. Yet she persisted. Powerful streams of suspicion fell on me. The green walk light in the other direction began flashing the insipid hand of red as a warning that the relief of this awkward moment was immanent. Her body language was screaming at me to leave her alone. Then it happened again.

As I turned to gauge the length of this interminable wait and looked to the flashing red hand which had caught my amazing peripheral sight, I noticed, that just a few degrees further to my right, she was there.

Now, I know what you are thinking. How could I possibly sneak one more look? You must place yourself in my spot, however, to appreciate the titillation based upon a single glance at that moment. I had to investigate whether she was feeling as odd about the moment as I. To complete this strange little cycle, something fundamental was tugging at my sensibilities. Only a degree or two to the right, in an instant it could all be over. A quick flick of my eyes and I would know of how in the history of this woman's memory I might fair. My eyes could no longer hold their gaze on the flashing red symbol and slipped to the right. There, for only the slightest instant, yet an instant that rent me to my very being, were the eyes of the woman. Eyes that had moved from a sort of suspicion to those that carried a validated fear.

What was I to do? She was obviously headed in the same direction. Could I force my legs to continue, or would I simply fall to the cruel, cold cement in the fetal position and live forever under this dubious cloud of false accusation? The mercy of passing time finally brought the green symbol of motivation. I stepped off the curb slowly, in a sideways manner, a shrewd maneuver that allowed the frenzied young female to go ahead of me. The sky no longer seemed blue. The sweet air was suddenly thick.

Pretending to be lost in the fascination of picking at one of my cuticles, I cogitated as to the best course. I could not turn around, not in the middle of the street. I would, therefore, continue across the street, shame in hand, and gather energy to move in whatever direction the disturbed young woman did not. Honor spoke to me that this was the only thing left to do. I owed it to my dignity to not accompany her further, even if it meant delaying my progress toward the daily chronicle and the steaming, rich black liquid which anxiously awaited me. She continued straight and I, proud yet heavy of heart, forced myself to turn left. Thus disengaging from the scenario of unrequited accusation, I left it all behind that hard, dank, brick building on the corner that had come between us.

Abandoned on the sidewalk, staring listlessly to the dirty pavement, I woefully plotted my next move. How was I to go on? The morning was shattered and its youthful glee wrung out of every petal on that cherry tree. It took a moment or two to gather my wits. Coming back from such devastation is hard for most. Yet I possess alacrity of spirit absent in most common men. As such, I shook myself out of my despondency and made a contract with myself to enjoy the rest of the day regardless of what had transpired.

By and by I found myself near those vending machines. Trauma was still present and it was difficult to look around. I slipped in my coins, listening to the gentle tinkle as they found their way deeper into the machine and wished that I too could find a tinkling trip to some sort of purpose. My legs somehow found the energy to shuffle toward my coffee.

All things of abysmal comportment, which take shape in our nature of existence as situations beyond our control, always have an ending. As if an exclamation point on the end of this endless, twisted, scheming horror created for me by an unfeeling god a shriek exited from my lungs. There, before my tearing, disbelieving eyes, sitting in the window of my humble cafe, was the woman who had ruined my day.

Some Seriously Superficial Invective

<hr>

(The stage is an urban back-drop of high rise buildings, restaurants, apartments and businesses one might see walking through any large downtown. The two protagonists will walk to center stage, left to right, and then begin walking in place. As they do so the urban scene will scroll behind them. People they pass will slide by with the background as if stationary to the two who are walking in place. Enter John and David dressed in business suits, carrying briefcases and well manicured)

John: How are you and the Mrs. getting along?

David: Terrible.

John: What now?

David: Oh, same old crap. She's still on that 'get-in-touch-with-your-feelings' thing.

John: Yeah, I really hate that crap. Don't even let her talk to Cheri. That would drive me out of my mind. After a long day at the office, let me tell you, I just want to be numb.

David: Well not Joni. Everything has to do with feelings. The only numb thing on her body is her skull. I tell you, this is getting serious. This feeling crap is going to drive us to divorce if it doesn't change.

John: I know. One sure way to screw something up the wazoo is to over-analyze it. Pick it apart. Feelings just happen. When they do they should be left alone, as far as I'm concerned.

David: I mean, how the hell am I supposed to get in touch with my feelings when there's somebody there waiting for them to come out. It's like somebody saying, 'OK, be funny now.' Or, 'OK, be sad now.' Feelings come out when they're supposed to. They're not like a dog programmed to bark when they want let out. Let out so they can go out and shit all over everything.

John: I think you got that backwards.

David: How so?

John: When a dog wants out, it barks. When feelings want out, they bark too. What Joni's doing is more like a command, like roll over, or sit, or heel, or shake.

David: Yeah, I guess you're right. I guess I got caught up in the shitting-all-over-everything part. I've been dumped on too much lately.

John: What you guys need is to be more systematic. Automatic. Look at what me and Cheri do. Five nights a week I know exactly what's going to happen, so does she and we get right on with it. We don't have to worry about *(with lugubrious emphasis)* '*feelings*,' or '*getting in touch*,' or none of that crap. When I get home Cheri's got my glass of wine on the table. We peck lips and she's on her way to the gym. I take care of Joey until she gets back. We get supper. We take turns putting Joey to bed. Then I read the paper; she watches television; we get ready for bed. And every Friday she ain't bleeding I get a quick poke. There, done. We're living our life. Dealing with it, with none of the head games that go along with it.

David: Yeah, well I already know what Joni would say. *(In a falsetto, mocking tone) You're not being spontaneous. You're not romantic. Tell me what you're feeling.* Jesus. What am I married to, a shrink? You want to know what she told me last night.

John: What's that?

David: She accused me of not appreciating anything.

(From the right, moving with the back-ground enters a homeless man. He is filthy, disheveled and sitting on the ground. As the audience see's the homeless man approach he raises a bowl to the two business men with a weak, grin)

John: Oh, don't let her start that.

David: Yeah, that's where I lost it. I completely lost it. I just looked her right in the eye and said...

(The two men stop walking in place near the homeless man and face each other, the back-ground and homeless man stop moving)

Look here. You don't think I appreciate anything? Let me tell you something. I bought every goddamned piece of furniture in this place. I bought that car sitting outside. I pay the bills that keep us in this house. You don't think I appreciate how hard it was to get all this? You're the one who don't appreciate anything--un-happy all the damn time.

(The two men begin walking in-place again, the scene starts moving and the homeless man moves off stage not noticed by the two)

John: Then what'd she say?

David: Oh, some kind of crap about knowing value as opposed to price; more new-age horse crap. *(David gives a small pause)* And then she tells me that she was talking about herself and not all the material things around her anyway. Right, just when you got them pegged and hung out to dry they twist it all around. Wenches, they were born to drive you nuts. If she is so obsessed with getting to her feelings why doesn't she ever get to the happy ones? The only feelings she ever gets in contact with are the miserable ones.

John: Cheri likes to twist stuff around too. The worst thing you can do is to give into it. Like a few weeks ago she started in with me on that you-don't-appreciate-nothin' crap. But I knew that she was talking about her and not the furniture and car and stuff, you know.

David: I guess that puts you way ahead of me. Not that that's a complement or anything.

John: It ain't. Anyway, it was Friday and time for bed...

(Moving in with the scene from the right is a prostitute dressed provocatively. She is smoking a cigarette and has a strung-out, washed-out look on her face. She is leaning against a lamp-post trying to get the businessmen's attention with short flicks of the head)

... So, you know, it was time to squeeze off the trigger and get some sleep. And then she starts in with it. Why not this? Why not that? So--stupid me--next Friday I get a baby sitter; we go out to a fancy dinner; we get home late and I'm tired. And, like she knows we do every Friday, I want to blow wad. *(Shaking head vigorously)* Jesus. Then it's 'go slow,' 'be passionate,' 'do this,' 'do that.' *(Exit prostitute)* She just hasn't figured out yet that, to men, sex is biological. Stick, grunt, snore. That's about all the feeling we want to put into it. But I take all this time to warm her up, wine and dine her, and she only wants more. Don't ever give in. Give them an inch and they want a mile.

David: That's no lie. It's like Joni quitting her job to have Joey. I give in and say 'OK' and it's all of a sudden permanent.

(On the scrolling back-ground a day care center appears)

What is it, almost a year now? Just how long does she want to sit on her butt? I don't think she appreciates how much overtime I have to put in to make ends-meat. A little work might help her peel off some of that lard she got while stuffing her face day and night while she was prego. She's still a pig and it doesn't seem like she cares about taking it off. Maybe I should get in touch with how I feel about being married to a fat slob. Speaking of work, how are things going? Has anything worked out?

John: It's a fucking nightmare. You wouldn't believe. I spend more time on the phone anymore than a 1-900 sex toy. Last week the boss tells us we're not getting bonuses this year because of budget cuts. They might even axe the annual dinner. Boy, now that's some incentive to bust ass.

(Enter with the scrolling scenery a man walking in place pushing a shopping cart loaded with recyclables. He is old, filthy, tired looking and bent at the shoulders)

David: I mean to tell ya. If there was a boss that knew anything about motivation I probably wouldn't begrudge busting my butt to work for him. Instead, it's a bunch of oppressive disincentives at every corner. They make it such a grind. We're barely getting any raise this year. But it's almost vacation time and I'll keep my sanity until then.

John: I think I'll just go crazy instead. What a nightmare.

(Exit recycler)

David: Anything in particular driving you nuts? Or is it everything in general?

John: Oh, the boss has lost his mind. He thinks he's colonel Klink and he's turning the office into Stalag 17. A new policy says anybody leaving the building has to sign out. Correction, everybody on our floor has to sign out. Nobody downstairs has to. You call that fair? Christ almighty...

(On the scroll enters a young black man leaning against the scene in 'spread-eagle' form. A large, white policeman is patting him down, pulling articles from his pockets, then begins hand-cuffing him)

... The guy's a moron. He's on our floor. He can keep an eye on us. Those downstairs people get to roam anywhere. I mean, even going out to get a doughnut, or a cup of coffee, we got to sign out. Now tell me, is that humiliating or what? Have you ever heard of anything so despotic or tyrannical?

(The officer pushes the hand-cuffed, young, black man roughly to make the exit from the stage. The two pedestrians stop and face each other again)

I just asked him, 'Hey, you mean I got to sign out even if I got to go pee?'"

David: What did he say then?

John: What do you think? You ask a reasonable question and he gets pissed off. I should just keep quiet and go along with all the shit just like every other butt-sucker in the office.

(They begin walking again)

David: Seems like the butt-suckers out number us any-more.

John: You got that right.

David: New guys are the worst. They're all minorities and women. I don't think we've hired a white male in two years. Well, there was Pensky. And Martin and... Hey, did I ever tell you about that other new guy, Johansson? He's crazy. We got to go have a drink with him some day. You'll laugh your ass off. He's hilarious.

John: OK, let's do it. *(Small pause)* Yeah, the only people hired these days are minorities and women. And all they talk about is this glass ceiling. Well, let me tell you, they aren't the only ones with a glass ceiling and I know who's on top of mine: women and minorities. I was talking to Paul about it, this minority hiring stuff, and he says...

David: Paul? How's he like the promo? He's almost a V.P. now, right?

John: Yeah, almost a Veep. That's going to be my only hope. Once he makes V.P. I'll be back on the ladder. He doesn't look for minorities or kiss-asses. He gets people who he can talk to and deal with. But who knows how long he'll last. He's an endangered white species too. Doesn't seem like anything is secure anymore. They work you. They milk you. And when they're through with you they throw you out the door.

David: You got that right. There's no loyalty anymore. You give and give and they'll go with someone else with a snap of the fingers.

John: No trust either. Like this sign-out thing. Nobody trusts anybody. You earn trust everyday for years and it means nothing.

(Enter a beautiful woman with the scenery, walking in place, well dressed, and with large breasts)

David: You'd think that loyalty and trust would build up over time. But not in the good old American work place. There's no such thing.

(The two men grow quiet and exchange a glance as the woman passes them. After a second or two they both turn their heads to take in a gratuitous stare)

John: *(letting out a low whistle)* What I wouldn't do for a piece of that.

David: Yes sir. If Joni had a set of hooters like that I'd be gettin' in touch with my feelings; I'd want to feel all day.

John: Yeah, if Cheri wants appreciation let her sprout a couple of them. Bet that thing wouldn't need a dinner to loosen up a crotch.

David: *(looking at his watch)* Oh well, late again.

(On the moving scenery comes a building with a huge clock on it. David removes his watch and places it in his pocket)

I'll just tell the boss I forgot my watch and didn't know what time it was.

John: *(Ponders for a second, then removes his also)* Sounds like as good an excuse as any. Who cares? Only butt kissers get there early. Like that Espinoza guy. Always early and he's always staying late. Waste of damn time.

David: Yeah, I got this Ms. Li Chan who is early every damn day. Now the boss expects it of everybody. Goddamn ass-kisser. And this new Mustafa boy down in the mail room--another affirmative action refugee. He runs errands on his lunch hour. Can you believe such brown nosing?

John: Mustafa, huh? One of them black Muslims?

David: Oh, you got that right. Mr. Big Black Militant Man, he wears that stupid hat and everything.

John: Why do they do that? When did everything start revolving around somebody's culture? *(In a mocking tone) Ethnicity? Diversity?* Everybody's so damn defensive. Every spic, bitch, nigger, and wet-back is looking to ram their ethnic background down your throat, screaming 'Respect me, respect me.' I respect them without all that crap. In fact, I would respect them a lot more if they didn't keep acting like some spic, bitch and nigger by demanding all that stuff.

David: I know what you mean. It's like they're living in the past. Someone ought to tell the son of a bitches that there is no more segregation and that they're getting advantages way beyond what we get.

John: I guess you can't blame them. If I was a bitch, spic or nigger I would want a free ride too. Everybody wants a free ride. Nobody wants to take responsibility for anything.

David: You've got that right. Nobody wants to take responsibility for anything. Just stick out your hand and gimme, gimme, gimme...

(In from the right comes a man lying down, propped up by one arm. He has a large wound on the side of his cheek and another on his head, both bleeding profusely)

...gimme, gimme, gimme.

John: Yeah, everything is falling apart and everybody else is supposed to pick up the tab.

(The two grow silent and avoid the stare of the wounded man who is now

reaching out a hand to them. As they pass, the wounded man cries out to them)

Wounded Man: *(weak and breathless)* Oh god, help, oh god help me.

(The two pedestrians. pick up their pace and the scenery speeds up pulling the man out of view)

David: *(throwing a thumb behind him)* what happened to that poor slob?

John: Wow, looks like somebody kicked the living crap out of him; holy cow.

(The two exchange glances and begin snickering)

John: Somebody put the thump to that boy.

David: Completely fucked him up.

John: Where were we? Oh yeah, nobody takes the bull by the horns anymore. You know, back in the good old days that stuff didn't happen.

David: You really think so?

(As John starts his monologue the scrolling scenery begins to take on a surreal look and fades into a moonscape, with a strange colored sky, and odd, extra-terrestrial dwellings)

John: Sure. People back then had some real dignity. There was no such thing as a free-loader. People pulled there own weight. That's why we were so much more prosperous then. There was no dead weight dragging us down. With everybody pitching in, you could raise a family on one income. Without having to support all these illegal aliens the schools could teach with out having to spend all their time worrying about Spanish. People walked taller in those days. Nobody went hungry. People got along. There was hardly any crime. No wife beating, incest, and sick stuff like that. Nobody hated anybody because everybody was a part of making things better. America was one, big, contented family--that was way back before you could make a living on the welfare state.

(As David starts his monologue the scene starts fading back to reality)

David: I'm not so sure I share your rosy view. I mean, things were better, but not pristine white. Look at my old man and mom. I was a bastard. I was conceived in the back hold of a fishing boat en route to Catalina Island. Of course my parents never told me that. My uncle told me. One night when he was real drunk he told. That was the same time he told me he had spent time in jail for statutory rape. He said that it was a plea bargain down from full rape. So, things weren't perfect. Just better.

John: All right. I'll grant you that. But back then people knew where and how to affix blame. And when blame was on themselves they knew how to take it like a man: Holy shit. Who today knows how to take any blame...?

(Two workmen carrying a large mirror enter stage right. They move until they are even with John and David. As they pause to adjust their grip on the mirror, David and John also pause in front of the mirror so that their reflection is displayed for the audience)

...anymore these days? I mean, who is going to stand up anymore and say something like, 'I'm at fault for this and that.' Really. No way. No-one does anything like that anymore. Certainly no damn politician. You know, so much for a nation of the people, by the people, and for the people.

David: You got that right.

(Workmen complete their rest and move on. The two protagonists begin

moving also. Enter two young women from the right. They walk up to the two protagonists and confront them. David and John try to sidestep them to no avail)

John: What the hell is this? Who are you two?

Woman 1: We're, kind of like, two concerned citizens.

David: What do you mean, 'kind of like'?

Woman 2: Well, to be more honest, we're actually members of the audience.

(David and John exchange a long, smirking glance)

David: You guys can't come up here. Get real.

Woman 1: Normally no, but we talked it over and decided to try and let you guys know just how shallow and stupid you're looking. And you're looking that way in front of a lot of people.

Woman 2: We didn't think it was really fair. I mean, they're portraying you as a couple of Neanderthals. It's not really very balanced.

John: *(agitated and jabbing an index finger close to the nose of woman 2)* Let me tell you something, little missy. What most of you women today have forgotten is that the world isn't fair. There is no little nirvana where everything is balanced out. You don't get hand outs. You don't get promotions because you got tits. You don't get things you don't work for. Understand?

Woman 2: *(shrugging shoulders and backing up)* OK, whatever. We thought we were doing you a favor.

John: When we need a favor we'll ask for it.

(The two women walk around the protagonists and exit the stage. John and David follow them out with a sneer and then resume their walk)

David: *(snickering)* What a couple of bitches those were. I mean, real, big, horrendous, snarling bitches. I guess you told them where they could stick their fairness crap.

John: You got to call them as you see them. Like I said if you give them an inch they take a mile. If I would have been nicey-nice they would have gone on for another two days. But stop it right there and no more trouble.

David: Wow, what a couple of in-your-face, full-on bitches. What do they know about fairness? They're probably on AFDC and I'm paying their bill. How about that for fairness?

John: What is this world coming to when a couple of welfare wenches can come up to a couple of hard-working tax-payers and talk about fairness? It's free-loaders like that who give taxes a bad name.

David: Yeah, my boss threatened to dock me time if I came in late anymore but I told him, 'So what, all it means is I'll pay less in taxes.'

(As John begins his monologue the scrolling scenery will produce in succession a school, a library, a police station, a fire station, a National Guard armory, a courthouse and a city jail)

John: Just what the hell do they do with all that money anyway? All they're doing is giving it away to welfare cheats like those two bitches and fat salaries to bureaucrats. Name me one constructive thing that my tax dollar has done in the last ten years and I might not fight paying them so damn hard. Go ahead, name one damn thing that my taxes go to that is worth a shit.

David: Don't ask me. I just pay them and hold my nose when I do so.

John: Damn right. These greedy politicians are just eating this country up. I pay, and pay, and pay and all they do is spend, spend, and spend.

David: You've got to get some better write-offs like me. Like that resort deal on Maui. Now that's a killer. I pay for a minimal interest in the resort and every time I fly my family there I write it off as business.

John: Yeah, I need something else to write off. It doesn't seem like I can take the family out to eat enough to manufacture a decent write-off anymore.

David: Yeah, you've got to be aggressive. Those bureaucrats will figure a new way to take it just as soon as you find a new way to squirm out of it. Bureaucrats and Washington, they're ruining our country; Blah, blah.

John: You've got that right; Big government, hack, snort, I'm indignant.

David: Blah, blah, taxes, whine, snivel, blame with outrage, bureaucrats. Gaggle, gaggle, glip, glop, cant and twaddle for a few more rhetorical moments.

John: Congress bliggle, the President blaggle, the deficit bloogle, snort some more and blame, blam, bloom, blum. Bluster, bluster 'til I'm flustered.

David: *(waving arms and briefcase wildly, screeching)* Miggle, maggle, liberal muck, flap my arms like a fucking duck.

John: *(both men stopping to face each other and saying in unison, while pointing a finger at each other)* you've got that right.

David: *(walking again)* I mean what the hell. We're destroying the American dream. People used   to be able to come here and make a living...

(Enter two Hispanic men, dressed casually, making small talk in Spanish)

... But not anymore. The American dream is dead. I mean completely dead, in the grave and molding, just like John Brown's body. My great grandfather must be spinning in his grave to see all this that has come to after braving Elis Island.

John: *(after the two men have passed)* Stinking wet-backs. They're everywhere. Now that's a big part of what's sinking our country.

David: You got that right. I can't get a goddamn cab with an English speaking driver anymore. And all of those convenience store operators gabble on in some kind of mush-mouthed accent and language. Christ, the last time I was in Montreal I must have walked around for an hour before I heard one word of English. All you could hear was nothin' but Mexican.

John: *(After small pause and a perplexed gaze toward the audience)* that's French.

David: What's French?

John: The language, Montreal's a French speaking province.

David: Oh, well, they live in an English speaking country don't they?

John: Yeah, but, see, I don't have anything against foreigners speaking something other than English in their own country. I mean, they damn well should learn English before they get here. But as far as speaking some kind of language where they are, hey, that's OK as far as I'm concerned.

David: Yeah, I guess so.

John: But back to the subject. We're falling apart. We're so screwed up. We don't have any rights anymore...

(As John goes through his monologue the scroll will fade into pictures of third world dungeons, executions, and tortures. Finally, it will fade into pictures of the holocaust)

...the government has taken over everything. Why not get pissed off? There's nothing you can do. The only damn person with any rights anymore is a goddamned criminal. I should become a criminal. It's the only way I'm going to get any rights. It's the only way to get ahead. Criminals make money, get slapped on the wrist and live like kings. We should shoot the bastards. Instead? Instead we give them a thousand appeals and let them free on every stinking technicality you can imagine.

David: Yeah! Now I'm getting in touch with my feelings. Screw the system. White males are the ones being oppressed. It's like a goddamned dictatorship. We don't have any rights any more; we gave them all to the wet-backs, bitches, niggers and spics. Work feels like a goddamned death camp. I'm just standing in line waiting for my turn to get knocked off. No shit, it's just like a fucking death camp. A death camp run by a bunch of spics, niggers and bitches.

(The two are silent as the scroll fades back to a city scene. On the scroll appears a California Department of Motor Vehicles. The two men stop in front of it)

David: Well, here I am at Stalag 17. It's time to check in with the guards for roll call.

John: You think you've got it bad. At least you can go get a doughnut without having to be under Gestapo surveillance.

David: It's been good talking to you John. One day America is going to wake up and smell the coffee and figure out what to do with all these filthy, money-sucking, bureaucrats.

John: You got that right. And if they don't, it's time to buy a bigger gun.

(David walks up to the scrolling screen and taps on it)

David: *(puzzled)* Hey, this is just a canvass.

John: What?

David: *(feeling around some more on the background)* well I'll be damned. None of this is real at all.

Reading Hemingway

"I love this guy. Just when you think he's going to drivel on interminably he throws out one of those little gems of dazzling insight that leaps off the page and into your common human experience. Just listen to this: 'Finished,' he said, speaking with that omission of syntax stupid people employ when talking to drunken people or foreigners. 'No more tonight. Close now.' Only Ernest Hemingway could have the clout and wherewithal to characterize someone talking down to a drunk as stupid. You've got to love the guy."

The lounging man reached over the side of the bed to get his snifter of cheap brandy. He continued in between short, delicate sips that far overstated the low caliber of the liquid. "And you have just got to be drinking when you read him. And not just anything, it wouldn't be appropriate to drink something like beer while reading Hemingway. I mean, I'm sure Hemingway had his share of beer but he doesn't really personify that sudsy, malty style. You know what I mean? It isn't that he couldn't identify, or fit in with that macho, sweaty, beer-on-tap, guzzle-in-a-bar wharf rat kind of scene. I just think he's removed from it."

He set his drink on the carpet with exaggerated grace and adjusted his small reading lamp so that the spot fit better on the page which was resting on his hairy belly at an angle. "I think that Hemingway is, kind of, beyond beer really. It may sound funny, 'beyond beer,' but I think it's true. If his characters were beer swillers, he would be inside that kind of scene looking out. Beer is a beverage of fraternization and not observation. Hemingway didn't sit inside a scene like beer sits inside a group conversation, there, sitting in the middle of the table, in a big pitcher that everybody pours from. Or coming from a common spout, hundreds of cracked and greasy mugs held under the same source. Hemingway was a sit-in-the-corner type of writer; a sit-in-the-corner, with a lone, special, bottle, sitting in the torment of the tropical heat and malaise, veiled by a dark shadow kind of writer. Off, away from the lights of public observation, a drama is played out, watched by the thoughtful, calculating eyes. A young Spanish maiden talks non-sense to her muscular and jealous suitor playing with his emotions, twisting his essence around a delicate finger and laughing out-loud.

"Beer breeds sincerity, an arm over the shoulder, a drunken song staggering to and fro to the beat. Hard liquor inspires that sort of ham-handed, smarmy, black-tuxedo, hair greased down, slap-on-the-back, kind of insincerity that displays the mordant side of life which can be juxtaposed against true and pure passion. A beery sot would already be half passionate and, by usurping a bit of sincerity, destroy the contrast in scenes.

"What do you think dear?"

His wife had already let her magazine drift flat on the quilted spread, her head pointed to the ceiling in the large, white pillow. "Well," she said sleepily, "a lot of his characters drank wine. Like everybody in 'A Farewell to Arms.'"

The man scooted up onto his pillow a little higher to sit nearly up right. He pushed one eyebrow low and the other higher swelling with the newfound conundrum and pondering its resolution. He snatched up the brandy, more brashly than before, catching the stem neatly between his four fingers, and swirled the brown liquid inhaling deeply its vapor. "Ah yes," he said pressing an index finger to his lips. "But that was in Europe. You must realize that I'm talking from a purely American perspective. In Italy, everyone is passionate to an American. From that perspective you can juxtapose against any sort of hard drinking."

The snifter went up high and the last of the burning liquid went down his throat. He fumbled for, and found, the bottle with its tin, screw top. He poured out a healthy shot, screwed the lid back on, and then smacked the top of the bottle with the palm of his hand pressing in the imaginary cork that fit his mind-set. "Really," he went on between more liberal sniffs and snorts, "Hemingway personifies Americans in the world. What is more an American archetype in the world at large than that of an overbearing, oaf of a man, talking loudly and stupidly, with that omission of syntax, to a foreigner? You can just picture some huge Texas millionaire pasting back the ears of a slight, genteel, French waiter, leaning over him with his hot breath, demanding a bottle of watery, American lager over a fine wine. 'No, no. Me, beer. Go now. Get beer.' Can't you just picture that Honey?"

"Mmmm-hm, yeah," came the voice, face hidden from view in the bulges of the pillow.

"I mean, Hemingway really turns the tables on them. The person on the receiving end of baby talk isn't stupid. It's the one doing the baby talk who is stupid. Really, when you're drunk you don't suddenly become stupid. You're drunk and nothing more. People act as if you've lost your faculties. People, that is, who don't really know what it's like to be drunk. I can just picture some tape-on-the-glasses, booger-dribbling bellhop walking up to Ernest Hemingway and saying something like, 'Finished. No more tonight. Closed now.'"

The man took in a large sip and breathed heavily through the nose while he swirled the cantankerous liquor around his mouth imagining it a fine, French, Napoleon Cognac. A sort of pride filled liquor, distilled from the bloody fields of France through years of toil under hard Nazi boots. Put into the bottle for a time when its drinking could be done with a head held high, as if encapsulating the best of France out of reach of the Nazi over-lords, it cheated the conquerors out of the best of spoils. It was the sort of liquor that ended up in the writer's glass as he toasted the liberation of Paris. The glasses go high. "Vive le France," comes the cheer from a crowded bar.

His little fantasy faded from view more quickly than he wished and he continued. "His characters drank a lot but he seldom characterized them as drunks; at least not hopeless ones. What was that he called them in 'Islands in the Stream'? It was, uh.... honey? What was that he called them?"

He gave the lump in the blankets a bump with the elbow. "Huh, what?" his wife said raising her head off the pillow to look toward her husband.

"What was that word Hemingway used to describe his characters in 'Islands in the Stream?' Do you remember?"

"Darling, Hemingway used lots of words." She lowered back into the pillow disappearing again.

"I mean, he didn't say the word 'drunk' to describe them. He said something else. What was that?"

"Oh, it was 'rummy.'"

"That's right. He said they were rummy. Now that fits. A drunk is someone who can't help but be there. A rummy is a person who goes by choice. Fed up with the niceties that mask true human turmoil disillusioned by the controlling entities of society, rummy retreats to a bar to simply obliterate it all and observe. A rummy doesn't retreat from society because he can't handle it, like a drunk. He retreats because he has already wrapped his arms around the futility of it all. He retreats for a vantage point, to poke fun, to have the last escape from hopelessness in the form of humor and satire. You won't find a rummy in a neighborhood bar with the same old yucks and chums who harbor such a place day in and day out. A rummy can be found in saloons with creaking floorboards, perched on a cliff over the Costa Brava, on moonlit nights, breathing the salt air and dreaming of a time when the innocence of youth masked the reality of cynicism. And out on the calm sea the moonlight streaks a path of invitation into the dark waters of the unknown. There our rummy can sit and sip, with his crusty, sardonic exterior protecting what is left of that innocent, disillusioned child inside."

For a moment, the bulbous snifter in the hand of the man became a small shot glass. In front of him there was an old table, with a dusty half-filled bottle of brandy. He was sitting on a splintered wooden chair whose joints were just loose enough to exaggerate any tipsy state. The corner was dark. A ceiling fan creaked, pushing the heavy, muggy night air. Across the room, at the far end of the battered old bar a young, dark-haired woman with a curled lip stood, her rounded buttocks moving muscularly under the silk of a dress that dipped too low for a good girl. She blew out a puff of smoke along with a few sharp words in her Latin tongue. Red lips sprouted surly from her smooth brown skin, which shone copper in the yellowish light of the storm lantern. She spied the American watching her. She turned and made toward him. Both contemptuous and voluptuous her legs slid back and forth until she was standing in front of him. "American," she said breathlessly from a heaving chest, a tongue running across white teeth, "you do not know me. Why do you stare?" The hard, grizzled, weatherworn man pulled the cork from the bottle and refilled his glass. He looked up into the glaring, fiery and beautiful eyes and, for just an instant, he believed that they saw something behind his disengaged exterior. In the flash of a moment, as dying embers scatter while being quenched, he thought there was a connection of souls. And then... and then...

His wife let out an exceptionally loud snore that shook him from his dream. He got up and turned off his little reading lamp, walked around the bed and turned off his wife's. Down the long carpeted hall he walked until he came to the large living room. He put his hands on his hips and studied the silence. He walked to the front window and pulled back the blinds to peak outside. The porch lamp illuminated the mown, sod yard and coiling walkway, which led up to the front door from the street. The street was wet with dew.

He stood thinking about the house, the car, and his job at the firm. He thought about his financial commitment to things -- the house and car -- and how they necessitated his continued labor at the firm, and how one was inextricably linked to the other. The connection seemed profound to his rummy mind.

"How I wish I was there," he whispered in grandiloquent conclusion. "God, I wish I was on the high seas."

Gold

Pastels were the only colors. There was no black or white. There was nothing but pale shades operating in a vague haze which gave hue to a pale life. Dark colors sat in front of Karl, but he refused to see them. There was a time when he saw stark color, but now everything had faded to a bleak and a dull sort of mosaic of life. Nature no longer had color, people had no color, and when people did express ideas about stringent color, it seemed everyone used it against him. He wandered off into a daydream thinking of what would happen if everyone on the planet earth were of the same color, spoke the same language, and showed respect for each other.

Piles of old venom spoke to him, as if freshly spewed by the snake of the vox populi he knew. Years of devotion in the third world, working with Africans in Africa, and other races in other countries, crossed his mind and then the word 'racist' invaded his scull, pushing away the snake of venom and taking precedent. People still had the temerity to call him a racist even though he had spent time in Africa, played football with black men, Mexican men, and white Americans. This bile ate at him, and had him looking to black. He tried to drift away from the black of his mood by staring at the pale blue walls of his apartment. Calm came to him eventually but these ideas were still knocking at the back door of his brain.

The word racist would come out of people's faces when he spoke candidly. He would tell people that he hated the term African-American because most black people from the United States have never been to

Africa and do not realize how they would be treated if they did go. Karl had seen how black Americans had been treated in African countries, and it was worse than he was treated while he was there. Questions rattled in his mind. What would you call a person from Morocco? What would you call a person from Egypt? What would you call a white person from South Africa whose family has been there since the sixteenth century? Karl didn't know why he was supposed to be a racist based on his honesty, but the vitriol he encountered seemed to transcend conversation with most people. He stared back at the pale blue wall.

Thoughts of his travels around the world entered his mind, easing the blackness of thought, and brought out the light, soft, and comfortable colors of life. The thoughts of the light hues eased his mind while he got ready to board the plane. He was on his way to the funeral of an old friend, but tried not to think of it as he drifted down the walkway to the entrance of the plane. The stewardess was pretty and perfunctorily polite. The seat was too small for a large man like Karl, but he squeezed into the window seat after clumsily slinging his small bag up into the compartment over him.

Everything hurt. Vertebrae in his neck had been fractured, ligaments in his knees torn, which made him waddle up and down stairs, and the dislocated shoulder constantly gave him trouble. Feeling all this pain, at this moment, he wondered if it had all been worth it. Death was final, and who would remember him after he was gone, let alone anyone while he was still alive. The silver medal for wrestling in the Olympics had taken years of suffering, thousands of hours of study, and the loss of his first wife for being so obsessed with his trade. He saw a vision of his ex-wife, then a vision of his struggle at the Olympics, then nothing at all as he closed his eyes.

The rim around the window of the plane was a gentle ecru. Karl opened his eyes, looked out to the runway and observed the black asphalt. He pulled down the shade of the porthole, a plastic shade which was a light brown in color, and it shut out the black of the asphalt. He stroked the cover with his left hand, almost in a state of wonderment. It was possible, he thought, to shut out all the nonsense of life. Shutting his eyes again, shutting them just as he had shut the plane's portal, he drifted off into an uneasy sleep during the delay to liftoff.

In his dream, he found himself back on the bright red mat, twisting and turning, and clawing with his sweaty opponent. A silver medal, that's what he had won. For his reward he had gotten disfigured ears, a broken body, and disdain for not having won the gold medal from friends, family, and the media. In the finals, the Russian man he was wrestling felt like he had some sort of oil on his body. Karl couldn't get an appropriate grip on any part of his body without it slipping through his hands. Time and again, the Russian man just slipped away and scored a point. The end of the match was rated eight to one in favor of the Russian. Even though he was in this uneasy doze, Karl heaved out a sigh of relief realizing his soul pointed to the pride that he hadn't been pinned.

A jostling came from the side and the old wrestler snapped out of his slumber and yelled, "Damn greasy bastard!"

"Whoa," said the sharply dressed young man who had plopped down next to Karl and had jostled him from his sleep. "I'm just taking my seat. I didn't mean to startle you. My name is Fredrick." He reached out a hand and Karl took it for a limp shake. "I'm into soybeans." The young man said with a grin. "That is I sell them on the market. Futures in soy are going through the roof and I'm making a fortune. My dad, in Iowa, used to grow soy beans but he never made the money I am making. If he hadn't lost the farm, he would be making a fortune by now." He continued in rapid fire bursts of monologue with a stretched grin. "But I only sell things that I know will make people money. Money isn't bad. Money makes the world go round." He raised his eyebrows and stretched his eyes wide. "No-one can tell you that I'm a dishonest business man. Here's my business card." He reached into his fine jacket and produced an embossed card and handed it to Karl.

Karl gave the card a cursory look then slipped it into the chest pocket of his pale blue polo shirt. Softness, he thought looking at his shirt, softness is the only thing left worth living for in life; Softness with gentle hue. He thanked the young man for his card and then leaned over toward the window, closed his eyes, and let out another sigh, and drifted into another uneasy sleep.

The year was 1968. The venue was Mexico City. He and his teammates spent the majority of their time in the Olympic village. It had a carnival atmosphere. Everything they needed was there. There was nice housing, American fast food, and the chance to meet people from other cultures. However, Karl and his teammates, between practice sessions, took the opportunity to make a few forays into the town to discover the local cuisine and culture. On one of these excursions, the group of six young men had found a brothel. They had been guided there by the one Hispanic on the team who spoke Spanish and had asked locals about the place. Business was booming in the brothel since the Olympics. All went in except for Karl, who sat on a dirty wooden bench outside. He was quite disgusted with his teammates. He knew two of them were married. Suddenly, a mouse ran across his feet, and across the sidewalk and into a drain.

The mouse stirred Karl out of his mood and he looked across the busy street. There was a man pushing a food cart. It had two large wheels, similar to bicycle tires, with a chrome plated handle on the back. He had never seen anything like this where he had grown, or ever anywhere he had been in his travels. There was a large red and white sun umbrella whose stem was planted in the front of the cart. Karl thought this was odd as it was only giving shade to the front third of the cart and not the sweating man doing the pushing in the heat of the day. Also notable to Karl was the detail of decoration on the cart. There were swirls of bright red, stabs of bright yellow going through the swirls, and a full spectrum rainbow glowing over the top. In the back, near the pusher, was a plastic decal of the Mother Mary, which shimmered in the hot sun. Her hands were pressed together, palm to palm, up near her chin and had her eyes rolled up heavenward. She had on a bright blue dress and there was a glowing yellow hallo over her head. The older man, the pusher, dark brown in complexion, with a large graying moustache, let the back of the cart fall to the pavement.

Karl, intrigued by the bright images on the side of the cart, went across the street to inspect the cart more closely. Crossing the road he had to dodge some busy taxis which were roaring by, belching out bluish smoke, and made it across the street to the cart safely. Curiously in this very hot day the cart proprietor had on a large, white apron, drooping around his neck and tied at the back. The apron was stained and the chubby older man wiped his hands free of the oil across it, leaving a few more stains from what was on his fingers.

"Que paso Senor? Asked the cart pusher to the well muscled American.

There was a menu taped to the back of the cart. It had quite a variety for such a small cart: tamales, burritos, tacos, and some sea food tidbits. Karl felt hungry, but was against any sea food in a cart. While Karl read the menu, the proprietor pulled out a cord from the side of the cart and plugged it into a local house. A heat lamp came to life, glowing reddish, over a pile of meat which was in a tray directly beneath it. The heat lamp was in the underside of the umbrella. "Two tacos," he said, then corrected himself holding up two fingers. "Dos tacos."

He navigated the busy road one more time holding the two tacos and sat down on the dirty wooden bench. As he ate, he thought about his teammates in the brothel. He wondered about paying for sex. He hoped he would never do it, and wondered as to why young, good looking athletes would feel the need to do so. The thought of how much it was worth for a young woman to sell her vagina to a stranger. The question of what the cost was came to mind and the image of seeing money change hands made him twitch. The sun was hot, and he took another bite of his second taco while a dusty wind swirled around the bright cart.

Karl's friends exited the brothel almost in unison and went to the obligatory joking and bragging about their exploits. Karl finished off his taco without comment. The hubris of his teammates bragging about their exploits left him speechless. They left the dusty bench behind and went toward the Olympic compound. The breeze began to lessen as they walked and Karl tried to ignore the comments of his friends. The heavy weight of the group, a six foot two, two hundred fifty pound married man from Kansas, with brown hair, made light of what he perceived of Karl's shy nature about the incident of him entering the brothel. Karl grabbed him, spun him to one side, poked him in the chest, and said, "Immorality is immoral no matter where you are in the world."

It didn't take long that evening. The tacos bought and ate from the brightly colored stand started a track meet through his colon. He spent most of the night on the toilet, standing only long enough to pull up his pants, only to yank them down again. The morning would offer the finals of his Olympic match and this weighed heavily on his mind. It was the gold medal struggle and he was sitting on the toilet, wondering if the virulent diarrhea he was having had him drooping his internal organs into the bowl. He knew there were more important things in life right now, other than dehydrating on a toilet, but his body wasn't responding to his request for health. The cramps were horrid and he found himself rocking back and forth on the toilet.

The time of the match was eight o'clock. He showered and put on his gear. It was time for him to fulfill the dream of his life: a gold medal. After the shower he drank a quantity of water then, while brushing his teeth, naked, he shit a liquid brown on the floor of the bathroom. The mess was cleaned up with wads of toilet paper and the shower re-entered. As the hot water hit him, he could feel his energy leaving his body as assuredly as a spent sparkler which had spewed out the last of its life.

He knew he could have beaten the Russian wrestler if he had been well. The fatigue from the episodes of the night before kept him from having the snap and quickness he was used to. Wrestling is a competition of inches, if not millimeters. In every tangle on the bright red mat, Karl was just that millimeter behind his Russian foe. Just before the last tangle, when he was losing badly, the track meet started in his intestines one more time. One more time, he pinched up, locked up with his opponent arm in arm, and lost another point just before the horn went off for the end of the match.

Frederick, primping in his wife's compact and adjusting his bright red tie, noticed the ex-wrestler beside him was making noises. Frederick nudged Karl as he noticed he was starting to twitch violently in his sleep. "Hey, are you all right?" he asked.

The fog of yesteryear faded slowly as he came out of his slumber. Plans and designs for the here and now would not fade. Failed plans and failed designs in his life after his Olympic endeavors, which nearly everyone thought as a failure, would eat at him forever. There was the bankrupt business, the failed marriage, child who no longer acknowledged he was his father, and the sudden death of his good friend, which outlined the frailty of his own existence. As the fog of yesteryear faded, and pangs of the present struck him, he blinked his eyes and looked to Frederick.

"Did you want something?" asked Karl.

"You were like, twitching," said Frederick with his cheesy grin. "I didn't mean to disturb you. But I thought something was wrong."

The words 'something was wrong' bounced around in Karl's head. He looked to the light brown window shade, closed and rubbed his eyes. What was wrong? The mist of horrors past kept flashing through his mind. The vision of his friend in a casket came and went with all the feeling of a door to door salesman who hadn't sold anything. He loved his friend but was adrift at how to feel for him. There had been things he loved, and knew how to express it. There were the flowers in the meadow near his house in the spring. He would bend down and smell them, caress the petals, and leave them to be without picking them. There was the small Down's syndrome boy who lived in his neighborhood who used to call him Mr. Karl and would bring over slobbery treats of sugar coated candy. There were lots of things to love, which had gone away, and now lots of things to have wrong.

"Tell me," Frederick said with grin still intact, interrupting Karl's daydream, "what do you do for a living?"

Karl blinked his eyes one more time. "I used to be a wrestler. Then my business went under and now I'm doing nothing. Nothing is something I understand these days. Doing something has consequences and I have become content with doing nothing." He scratched the side of his face and then stared back at the light brown shade.

"Wow," the young man said, "I used to be a wrestler too." His smarmy grin stuck on his face and the bright red tie around his neck irritated Karl. "In high school I was considered one of the best. I had a match one time where I was really sick, but I still won. I ground it out and took one for the team. Hey, where did you wrestle?"

After a pause, Karl responded, "Quite a few places." Karl drifted for a moment to High School matches, college matches, and then to the qualifying matches for the Olympics. He then continued. "I guess the most notable was when I was in Mexico City."

"Mexico City," responded Frederick incredulously, gave a laugh then continued, "Oh, so you were one of those dudes with the masks who jumped around in some sort of choreographed stunts. That's admirable. Because those guys were the model for the US wrestling guys, the WWF, or whatever you call it."

The idea of being thought of as part of a choreographed shenanigan stung Karl. He scratched the side of his face one more time and said, in a tone as calm as he could muster, "I was in Mexico for the Olympics. I won a silver medal there."

Frederick kept the grin and said, "Well, we can't always get the gold. But I've got gold now: Soybeans. How about it? Would you like to invest in soybeans and finally win that gold?"

Sympathy for the Devil

I was listening to the birds sing. They weren't far away. You couldn't imagine how badly I wanted them dead. I had no use for such happy noises anymore. I had no fire under their vibrant notes. Their sweet titter just seemed to make me limp. My destiny peeled away under the stark glare of their innocence. The damned fluffy, feathery little balls of life would have been better squawking from between my knuckles. Sometimes they almost made me smile.

It was time to think about such things, I thought, while listening: That balance that is. How was it we came to all this good? What was it on the other side of the invisible fulcrum of reality that props up our hollow glee? Like a cantilevered window, was it hidden behind the panes while we enjoyed the fruits of its existence? Are the warm summer breezes, felt upon our faces, coming to us due to the exertion of a force through a cord to a place beyond our view? Away from all inspection it exists. A cold, damp, rusted lump of metal, suspended by its neck, it dangles in the sealed blackness. From the motion of the cord and the vibration of the runners it can only infer the sunlight and warmth beyond. Connected to, yet forever separated from the splendor of the light, this mournful entity writhes in unseen pain. Time after time, it pulls, through natural forces, down on the cord as if to try and suck some life to itself along the greasy rope from the world outside. It moves up and down time after time longing in horror for the joy that it is creating. Could it be, I thought, that reality itself is balanced, that our pleasure is somehow evened by someone else's pain?

It is hard to say how I came about to that state of mind. We listened, talked, drank and laughed over and over in a fog of casual bliss. It mattered who did what and where was that and who would do thus. We all seemed pointed in that one direction never looking back, forever plodding on, and never swerving from that damnable course. Were we all free and simply chose to follow? Or were we all slaves without the ability to question?

In the recesses of the mind there are such uncontrollable thoughts. It is there that we begin to discover how little control we actually exercise over our destiny. Down in the fissures of the sub-conscious you can really see how it is all laid out. Peeking into the crack, as a roach stuck in a trap might view the world outside, we see great expanses of space and time that lie beyond us. As we view we suddenly realize there are sickly vapors choking the life slowly out of each of us. It is within these fetid, sickly swollen trenches that the universe begins to open and the bitter fruit of knowledge slaps us in the face. We realize that by looking in we are looking out. We see, as our organs groan under the growing sepsis, that the universe lies beyond our control. As we are connected to the infinite, connected yet detached, the sunlight of life giving energy is within us all, yet removed.

Perhaps it was my seditious nature or maybe the penchant for chasing my fears. Why did I drive myself to such extremes? Who in all of eternity purveyed such enlightenment to themselves? It gnaws at me day after day with such unpitying pain. I just had to experience it though. Existence would have had no meaning for me if I hadn't pulled it close and tasted it like a forbidden lover. And I did. There, in the shapeless abyss, it caressed me with searing cold and blistering fire. I could hear the voices of those heroes who had gone before. They were mocking me, screeching hateful forms tearing at my decaying flesh they would not stop hating me. They ripped at the tatters with spiny maws until there was nothing left. Who among us would show such courage? Where would there be another who would not succumb to the siren song of the knowledge of eternity? Puritans smacking together their rosy lips would lose control of their bladders at the thought. What priest would withstand such a fury for the pulpit of right? I took the step of destiny without anyone pushing me. No-one was there to tie me to a stake. No-one was there to nail me to a cross. I had not these luxuries that have been endured by others in the name of pain and sacrifice. In the sullen gloom of the barren void I alone took the step and I alone bear the pain of touching the truth.

It is all a matter of balance. Push and shove action and reaction, hate and love each pair part of the universal pair which gives definition to our frail consciousness. As I turned away from the course that was, something came between. A thin veil of separation that was part of both yet belonged to neither. Within this boundary there came beings that resembled the boundary itself--beings of both sides, yet neither, with the ability to chose their own course.

There you all are, every one of you, close enough to feel my icy breath. You stumble this way and that on the tight rope, an inch towards me, then an inch towards them. Drunk with power you make pretenses toward each. Accursed fools! You don't deserve what choices you have and, once in a while, revenge is mine as I entice you over the edge.

It was such a cruel thing to do to one who was only seeking knowledge. Deprivation can only be paired with privation to have it fester. Here I exist at the interface of all earthly satisfaction yet am unable to draw one breath of sweet air. The warm bosom of a mother's breast is touching my face yet I feel no warmth. Crystal spring water drips off my tongue yet I am dying of thirst. Longing has given away to maniacal passion in my all consuming desires. God if I could just have one moment back I would touch the cheek of an innocent child and forever be satisfied at breaking the totality of this barren existence.

Beyond you accursed fools, who stagger about on the razors edge of reality, lay those most hated cowards. Light-years away yet just beyond the thin cellophane of the universe they frolic in the light. It is the light that blinds me into the blackness I see. Young, beautiful maidens dancing in bliss growing forever more joyful while I grow more sorrowful at this sight I cannot see. Familiar faces show me their charity with compounding empathy while I drive my mind to scratching at the outer edges of hate.

Bastards of Eden, where is your joy without my sorrow? Where is your love without my hate? I have come here of my own freewill and sealed my fate. Where is your sacrifice? Where is your pain? I am your sacrifice. I am your pain.

A Family Holiday

"Oh for Pete's sake, hurry up," dad yelled to no-one while leaning on the open door of his big, old sedan. He was directing his comments to the hole in the middle of the varnished rectangle that delineated the open front door of his house. The open orifice connected with his antsyness and probed a soft spot in his guts via his straining eyes. When no answer came, he began tapping his fingers on the blue roof and yelled again. "Darn it Sharon, it's already ten o'clock."

Sharon's head appeared at an oblique angle in the frame. "Bobby has to go pee," she said plaintively, letting the 'ee' in pee whine on in a disparaging tune. After hesitating a moment, blinking her owlish, blank eyes a few times to convey body language that she did not share her husband's parsimonious time-table, she disappeared back into the house.

Dad clicked his tongue and snapped his watch to attention in front of his face one more time. Ten o'five. Nothing, he thought, absolutely nothing gets done around here without a hernia first. Bright, white light reflecting off the white paint of the house burned its etch onto his squinting eyes leaving only the focus of the deserted aperture. Dad let the heat of the morning bake the back of his neck under his golf cap and it mixed with his sizable case of indigestion. Grinding molars locked his jaw tight and his brow puckered so tight it began to give him a headache.

To try and ameliorate his frustration at the delay he decided to go over, once again, his mental packing list. Without his planning, packing, and determination, dad thought, this trip would never, ever, ever, even get off the ground. Let me see: batteries, snacks, mosquito repellant, tent, stove, hatchet, water, sleeping bags, silverware, knife, poles, hmmmm... what else?

Dad wasn't particularly mad at his little name sake for having to relieve himself. He was angry at every little delay that had jumped in front of his efficacious, obsessed desire to be on the road before the heat of the day since dawn. The car had been packed for two hours now, with no help from the other three members of the family clan. All they had to do was to get up and get dressed. And now here he was, standing and waiting for that pineapple to be crapped.

Thoughts mixed with indigestion, heat and indignation, and he yelled again with exasperated emphasis. "Sharon! Let's get going."

Sharon's head appeared again, irritated, with orbicular eyes amplified by thick, square glasses. The short, limp blonde hair framed the white face in a way that infuriated Bob--he hated when she didn't do something to her stringy hair, anything. "Susan can't find her book," she said waggling her head in frustration in a way that further annoyed her husband.

"Oh for Pete's sake. We're going camping. She doesn't need her book." Then with heavy emphasis on each word, "Let's... get... going."

"Bob," came his name in a sing-song mewl, "if you could do a little more to help we could get going."

Do a little more to help? Thought a provoked, hard-working father, "Do a little to help?" snapped back that same patriarch parroting his thought. "What the hell do you think I've been doing since six o'clock in the morning? Who do you think packed this car? Who do you think got everything done?"

Sharon shouted back with enough emphasis to distort her high, nasal voice, "Don't shout at me! The neighbors will hear." Then disappeared again.

Dad reached up with both hands and adjusted his cap fussily as if preparing for a military inspection, his long, bony elbows sticking straight out from his parabolic ears. After the hat, both thumbs went down inside his belt to adjust the baggy trousers for battle. You want anything done right, he thought; you've got to do it yourself. He then stood back from the door and dramatically slammed it shut. Two long, purposeful strides took him to rounding the hood before he froze in his tracks with that peculiar feeling that grips someone who just realizes that they have just done something incredibly stupid. Something stupid done in the name of being indignant. He stalked back to the handle and gave it a futile yank. Locked. Inside he could see the keys swinging gracefully from the ignition, reacting to the force of the slammed door.

This was quite a pickle for stewing Bob. Now he would have to face Sharon having done something stupid. Something stupid for having been in a hurry, as she would surely point out while taking an extra hour to dither as penance for his stupid act. For a moment, wild thoughts of the possibility of finding a secret trap door into the family sedan crossed his mind, but they were squelched by reason, and the cold, hard facts presented themselves as irreconcilable. There would be no way out of admitting to Sharon he had locked the keys in the car. Stupid.

Bob crossed the threshold with a mixture of anger, embarrassment and defensiveness. The tiled entryway was clear, inviting him further into the confessional. No-one was visible across the carpeted front room and his reluctant legs glided on. Bob made his way down the hall towards the bedroom hearing strained voices and the clatter of last minute struggles. Pushing open the master bedroom he saw Sharon crouched in front of the vanity wielding a curling iron with hair pins in her mouth.

"Oh for heaven's sake," Bob said slapping his lanky thighs, all at once forgetting his embarrassment and the fact that limp hair annoyed him. "Can't that wait?"

Sharon pulled the pins out of her mouth and straightened up, startled by being caught in another delay. "Honey," she said recovering quickly in a feigned urgency that imitated his, "we forgot film. You've got to hurry down and get film. We'll be ready when you get back."

"We can get film on the way."

"Mom," Sharon heard her daughter squeal from one of the forward bedrooms, "Bobby's trying to write in my book."

Sharon used the convenience of the distraction to walk past her husband into the hall. "Bobby," she yelled, "give your sister back her book. Are you dressed yet?"

After a short pause, the daughter answered for her little brother. "No," she yelled vindictively, "he's just in his underwear."

"Bobby," instructed mom, "leave your sister alone and get dressed."

Bob added his paternal two cents. "Bobby, get ready now."

Then turned to his wife. "We'll get film at the store on East Avenue before the freeway."

Sharon replied on her way back to her hair job. "Just go now and we'll be ready when you get back."

"Just get ready now."

"I'm not ready now."

"Alright. Alright. But you better be ready by the time I get back. It's going to be nine hundred degrees in the shade by the time we get going."

Bob was half-way down the hall when the chill of remorse froze him in his tracks again. Keys. Damnit, keys. Bob stretched and put his hands on his skinny hips deliberating his options, which were nil, yet he deliberated nonetheless. Sharon's husband was a tall man with hard, bony features on his face which belied the mushy nature of everything south of the neck. He was one of those men able to pull off that incongruent morphology of being thin yet having a belly, soft as a marshmallow that protruded from under his concave chest. He irresolutely turned back to face his wife.

"Well?" she said pulling out her pins one more time. "What now?"

Plaintively and defensively, avoiding direct eye contact, he mumbled, "I need your keys."

"Where's yours?"

"I..." the pronoun came out, and then he faltered. "I... uh, locked them in the car."

Sharon's eyes lit up. She put her hands on her hips and bobbed her head up and down. "Why can't you ever learn? See what being in a hurry gets you?"

Bob prepared for military inspection again, hat and trousers, clicked his tongue and stuck out his hand waiting for the keys.

"Well you can't use mine," she said in a tone mixed with glee, vindication and parental instruction.

"Come on."

"You can't," she said relishing every syllable, "mine are in my purse and you so efficiently packed my purse in the car. This happens every-time."

"What happens?" Bob snapped trying to mount a credible defense.

"You get worked into a frenzy trying to push everybody out the door and it ends up taking ten times as long. If you would just help out we could get going."

Dad was really steamed now. The truth in her words strummed every exposed nerve like an out of tune banjo. "Like hell," he yelled. "I'm the only one who's been doing everything since six o'clock this morning."

Sharon, still playing to her advantage in the situation, put a splayed hand on her diminutive cleavage, stood back and lectured her husband in an even tone. "What you should be doing, besides using foul language on your wife, is figuring out how you're going to get your keys out of the car. Don't you think so?"

Bob's jaw snapped shut and he spun on his heels. This one was a no win situation and retreat was necessary. Foul language, he thought, you're going to hear some real foul language in a moment or two.

Down the hall a louder than normal scream erupted from his daughter's bedroom just as he passed the door. Dad turned quickly, motivated less by the playful wail than by the need to find someone to take his anger out on, and leaned into the doorway as it sprang open. Out from under his leaning torso shot his squealing, laughing daughter. Little Bobby was not far behind, holding his super-soaker, whose shot went high and wide right into dad's face. Bobby froze, paling; filled as full as any five year old could be with 'got-cha' guilt. Bugging eyes reflected the look on his father's face and his top lip began to quiver. Bobby dropped his gun and grabbed with both hands at the underwear around his crotch, biting his lower lip.

Bob senior drug a big hand slowly down across his dripping face. He raised a quivering index finger and pointed it at his shivering son. In a paralyzing, muted tone that never need be elevated to an offspring, a universal tone of dread, perhaps too angry to get loud, Bob heaved out, "The next time I see you, you better be dressed and ready to go."

Bobby rattled his head up and down as fast as he could then sprinted out of his sister's room under the towering wrath of his father. Little Susan was waiting for him at the entrance of the bathroom with an extended tongue, reveling in the fortuitous circumstances, doing a little hip-hoppy, happy dance from one foot to the other. Circumstances like this are offered so infrequently to older siblings that Susan was going to make the most of it.

Senior Bob did not look back until he was outside. Standing in the middle of the lawn, crossing his arms tightly, he took a deep breath and jerked his head back and forth on its spindly pole between the car and house trying to decide how to get the keys out. As his anger weakened to perplexity he cogitated, mused and scratched his head but nothing came to him. He walked over and peered into the window. Burglar proof latches on the door could be seen on the far side. The latch on his side was out of reach behind the angle of the window, though he pressed his face close to try and see where it might be. If it had been his old Pontiac, he thought, a hanger would have had him in and out in no time at all. It was just the thought he needed to redirect the anger at himself for having locked the keys in the car. "Sharon," he said out loud to him, "she's the one who wanted to buy this piece of junk." There was no longer any doubt in Bob's mind. He would have to get those keys out and make up for Sharon's folly.

Though he wasn't, Bob considered himself inventive and mechanically inclined. Possessed with this confidence, however, he did make for some valiant attempts. Borrowing little Susan's vanity mirror he leaned it carefully against the passenger side window. Returning to the driver side he could see the latch which was down below the window and previously out of sight. As he looked into the mirror Bob was feeling quite clever and lowered himself until he could see his smiling face to give it a congratulatory wink. He went into the house to fetch a wire coat hanger. Using a pair of pliers he unwound the hanger and bent a hook on the end. Carefully, trying not to scratch the paint around the window, he inserted the hook and the rest of the wire until it appeared in the mirror close to the latch. With a little bit of practice he mastered the backward seeming motion of the wire relative to the mirror and sallied forth in his endeavor full of confidence.

For the next forty minutes father Bob wrestled with a stretched out, wire coat hanger trying to work it under the locking latch. Sweat poured off of him; his hands continually lost their grip on the skinny piece of wire. The vexation which had moved down from its peak now soared to new heights. Like a long, thin spider's leg with extreme cerebral palsy, the wire danced to one side, then jerked to the other, then above, then below with predictable and maddening regularity, always missing the latch itself by precious millimeters. Twist this way and the wire would go above. Twist that way and it would go below. Slippery fingers strained to get enough force to turn the wire. Pull this way and it snapped behind. Pull that way and it jumped to the front. On and on it went. Each time the wire flitted past its appointed slot Bob would strain out his tongue to one side as if the tongue itself had some sort of psychic power to push the hook into place. The struggle continued.

At one point Bob bent over and used his teeth to try and get the proper torque. When the little bent hook just missed its mark again, he stood up and growled into the sky. He stared menacingly into the mirror; the wire was resting tantalizingly close to the edge of the latch. In a completely reflexive maneuver, Bob punched at the window with the fleshy part of his palm as hard as he could. The large mass of the car recoiled slightly but just enough. Bob saw the mirror--the cute, little vanity mirror, lined with horses, that he had bought for little Susan for Christmas, which had become her pride and joy--rock up from its slanted position and, in what seemed like slow-motion, fall to the ground. The crash and tinkling glass that followed rattled up and down his spine as he grit his teeth and sent his shoulders up around his sizable ears.

"Oh, damn. Damn it," he said rooted in his spot, too afraid to go and see the damage.

Just as he was formulating thoughts about how to get out of this one, he saw a form in the doorway. It was Susan. She had seen the crash and had both hands over her mouth. Bob felt himself shrink to the size of an insect. Before his brain could get an apology onto the palate tears appeared in Susan's eyes and she was on her way to seek recompense from a higher authority. "Mommy!" she wailed in utter anguish. "Mommy, daddy broke it. He broke it."

The sound of his daughter's howling lowered as it retreated and increased as it came back to the doorway dragging mother in tow by one, white-knuckled hand. Bob came around the car with both arms hanging limp, absolutely bewildered. He avoided the accusatory gaze of the oncoming siren by staring at the shattered remains of the mirror. Slowly the shrieking died down until it was nothing more than tearful burbling into the skirt of her mother, clutching desperately with both arms.

"What on earth did you do?" Sharon chided, patting Susan on the back.

Bob squat down and picked at the remains gingerly as if each shard were poisonous or cursed. He looked up into his wife's stern glare. "Well I didn't do it on purpose," he snapped and stood back up.

On the creamy white sidewalk that ran down the street appeared their neighbor, Jeff, coming out to see what the commotion was all about. He was a large, burly, beer-bellied man with black hair everywhere except where it was shaved. His over-tight, plain white t-shirt contrasted sharply with his dark farmer's tan. Because he was quite a lot of what Bob wasn't--big, strong and macho--Bob loathed Jeff, but rarely got a chance to show his contempt.

"How's everything goin'?" Jeff said in a prying way that annoyed Bob to no end. "What's wrong with little Susie?"

"Oh, Bob broke Susan's mirror," denounced Sharon, turning away from her husband and toward the neighbor.

Jeff ran his eyes from Bob to the mirror several times. "I didn't do it on purpose," snapped Bob again.

"I didn't say that," Jeff said. And after a pause, "Well, how did you do it?"

Bob felt his face flush. He half mumbled and half told the story which was told enough to send Jeff into gales of laughter. Little Susan whimpered through the entire tale. A fully dressed Bobby came out of the house toward the end of the narrative happy to see that his antagonist was busy with her own trauma. He joined in with Jeff's laughter until dad caught his eye with an evil glare that sent him clinging onto mamma like sister.

"Judas priest," cackled the barrel chested man. "Are you sure you ain't Oakie?"

Bob fumed under the charge. Jeff had a full shop in his garage and was always deriding the quality of Bob's work as 'jury rigging' or 'Oakie-fied.' "I suppose you got a better way to get in?"

Jeff pointed a thick index finger skyward, raised his eyebrows high and said. "I'll be right back."

After the neighbor turned to walk, Bob mumbled to himself, "Well don't hurry." He then turned to his turn-coat son. "Bobby," he said authoritatively, "go get a garbage can so I can clean this up."

As Bobby made the slow, reluctant peel away from mom's skirt and toward the house, he stuck a finger in his mouth; his pace resembled more a death march than that of an errand.

Sharon watched Bobby go then looked down at Susan who was stretching out the last, residual gurgles of the fit. "Don't worry honey. Daddy will buy you a new one right away." Then while looking at Bob, shaking a head up and down answering the suggestion, "Yes, daddy will go and get you a new one the same time he goes and gets us our film. He'll do that while we finish getting ready."

Bob knew that Sharon was playing events to the advantage of her stall tactics but there wasn't much he could do about it. He was stuck. Now it would be at least another hour. Toy-R-us, where the mirror had been purchased, was clear on the other side of town, and no parent ever got out of that zoo alive in less than forty minutes. Dad stared at the broken mirror trying to will it back together.

By the time Jeff returned, mom and Susan were already back in the house. Jeff brought with him this time a can of beer. Without a word to the fuming Bob he went to the driver's side of the sedan and produced a long, flexible, flat piece of metal with a notch cut on one end out of his back pocket and set his beer on the roof. With a tongue protruding from pressed lips he shoved the notched end down into the skinny space between the window and door. After only a few seconds of probing, the door popped open.

Jeff raised his can of beer towards Bob and said, "Cheers," and took a long drought.

Bob knew he should say something like 'thank you,' but it stuck in his throat. Instead, he managed an insincere grin and started rattling his head up and down saying, "Yep, yep, yessiree."

"Don't think nothin' of it," Jeff said, and then turned toward his house downing the rest of his beverage.

Bob wandered to the driver's side and wiped away the watery ring of where the beer had been sitting, inspecting close for some sort of damage to the finish. When, to his disappointment, there was none, he walked back to the broken glass. "Bobby," he yelled, "where's that garbage can?"

———————— ¢ ————————

Traffic on the way to the toy store was abominable. Every green light missed behind the long row of cars crawling to a start ground a little more enamel off of Bob's molars. Stop and go traffic on the freeway made him fantasize about helicopter-cars and tanks. Sweat poured down his face and the fumes of the idling cars filled his head until it throbbed. It was already ninety-five degrees, at least, and though it was too late to get going before the heat of the day the idea of doing so still chaffed at him incessantly.

The huge parking lot was not much better than the surrounding streets. People stopped dead in the narrow lanes waiting for a precious space to open stopping the flow from the street which stopped traffic on the road. Bob cruised the parking lot in a stop and advance manner until he saw and old couple getting into their car. He stopped in the lane to wait like every car he had just been cursing. After a while, a pile of cars were stopped behind him adding a litany of curses to heaven to follow Bob's. A few in the crowd began tapping on their horns while the old people prepared themselves, causing Bob to dispatch a few more curses to the Holy Ghost to follow the curses emanating from behind. Grandpa and grandma were indeed taking their time and Bob modified his curses accordingly; whatever the crises keeping grandpa from backing out was not apparent to him. A few more honks from behind, which went straight to Bob's stomach, winding up his innards even more tight than before and grandpa finally started a slow exit.

From the other direction there appeared in front of Bob, a little Volkswagen bug going the wrong way down the lane. Swinging out from the parking spot, the old man pointed his tail towards Bob's sedan screening him from the opening. As he cleared the spot, the car coming from the wrong direction slipped in between the old man's front fender and other cars parked there to steal it. Bob was furious.

Out of the Volkswagen appeared two young college kids. Both were lanky and long haired, one with an earring. Bob leaned out of his window and yelled, "Hey, what do you think you're doing?" The two gave Bob a bland look and kept walking. "Hey," Bob continued, "I'm talking to you. I'm...."

The old man had departed and the crowd behind was much more

interested in moving the pile than in castigating the two youngsters. Honking began in earnest drowning out the infuriated commuter.

"Damn kids," Bob muttered to himself. "Stupid, damn kids." Continuing his search around the lot, Bob went into a long and involved fantasy of what he should have done to the two 'punks' who had stolen his spot. Sharp kicks in the genitals, swinging them around by their hair, every mean thing he could think of went into the fantasy that, ironically, had no effect on the two perpetrators of the crime but significantly raised Bob's blood pressure.

Bob ended up finding a parking spot on the far corner of the lot. The air-conditioning in the store was refreshing. It even cooled his passions a little. He had not been in the store since before Christmas and found the crowd much more manageable today than the hoards he had fought in late December. He could hike the cavernous isles without much fear of being trampled. And hike he did.

Up and down, down and up, he searched in earnest for the little mirror with horsies on the trim. Occasionally, in a rare meeting, perhaps only a little more probable than a large meteor hitting the earth, he would find a sales person, one actually imitating work, and ask directions to the location of the mirror. They would either stare at him contemptuously, or give him false information and retreat to the 'Employees Only' section of the store. Whatever solace the air-conditioning offered was gone now and Bob started a slow jog up and down each isle huffing and puffing not from exertion but to show his testiness. Surely a tugboat with a fire hose on parade had less pressure coursing through it than Bob's throbbing arteries. Then he saw him.

At the end of one such huge ravine of children's toys he made out one of the figures whom he had trashed in his fantasies. The lanky, long haired fool who had driven the Volkswagen in front of him like a battering ram to steal his spot. All of Bob's visions of pummeling the young fool came back to him. The long, lean father found himself strutting up to the youngster, his fists clinched.

The young man was wearing a vest that signified that he was an employee of the store. He was busy doing inventory and didn't see the gawking customer stride up purposefully behind him. Over his left shoulder he stood, both fists clinched, his concave chest nearly making a convex angle. He stood there for nearly a minute until the young man heard his throat clear, once, twice and then a third time.

Looking back over his shoulder, lowering his inventory sheet, the young man asked, "Can I help you?"

Bob held his ground, head tilted up, and fists kneading themselves in an anticipatory fashion. In response to his adversary's question, he merely blew a sharp breath of air out of his nose.

Bewildered, the young man held an open palm out to the side. "Uhh, is there, like, something you need?" he asked.

Bob could feel his manhood pulsing now. He vibrated his head up and down a little. "Yeah, uh-huh, uh-huh," he let out between his clenched teeth and tightly stretched lips.

The young man shook his head slowly back and forth. "Do you, like, need help or something?" he asked again.

Bob let a snicker out through his nose in short, staccato bursts.

"Yeah," the young man said walking away, "like I'm going to get your... well, that stuff now. Like, right away." Then he disappeared into an 'Employees Only' swinging door.

Bob eventually found the mirror feeling particularly macho at having faced down his adversary. In his mind, it was as if he had out-dueled Medusa on a tight-rope over a pit of boiling oil and snakes. Everything on Bob's body tingled with a testosterone flavor. He was no longer a skinny, weak, beer bellied dork pushed around by the likes of Jeff. He had metamorphosed into a wiry, sinewy, cowboy on the prairie who had just beaten back a passel of Indians with his true grit. This cowboy, spurs a clankin' against the asphalt, strode up to his horse, package in hand, and shoved in the key.

When the horse or sedan as it were, didn't respond appropriately, cowboy Bob was incensed. He tucked the mirror under one of his long, saddle strong arms and gave the key a twist suitable for a branding-iron wielding sort of cowboy he had become. When this still had no response, Bob reared back, snorted and gave that dad-burn key a whole heap of his wrath and twisted the head right off in the lock.

Cowboy fantasies faded from his mind as quickly as a sonic boom echoes to the horizon. He held the stubbly end of what was left of the key close to his nose for inspection hoping it would grow roots and re-sprout another set of teeth. His ears picked up the fact that a low groan was coming from his throat. Suddenly, the spurs, cactus, cows and chuck-wagon of prairie existence faded to reality: He had broken his key off in the lock.

——— ȼ ———

"Mom," Bobby yelled from the screen door on the back of the house. "Mom." When there was no response, he screamed louder raising and lowering the tone in the stretched out noun, "Mom!"

Sharon pushed the mute on the television, just as disinclined to move toward Bobby as he was toward her. "What," she yelled back from two rooms away.

"I'm goin' out with Earl."

Sharon looked at the big clock on the wall. Her husband had been gone for more than an hour. She rolled her eyes. In the short delay between the question and response came another impatient, "Mom."

"Alright," she yelled, "but don't go out of the yard. Your dad will be in a hurry when he gets home." The screen door slammed well before she had finished her sentence. Sharon heaved out a large, irritated sigh. With a distracted push of a button, the volume returned to her old, out-dated, Saturday afternoon love story and Sharon tried to regain what dialogue she had lost.

Earl was Jeff's oldest son. He was the same age as Susan, seven and a half, but his father refused to let him play with girls. So, instead, he played with Bobby and the situation worked to both their disadvantages. Bobby was still too young and clumsy to play most any sport that might interest Earl. As a consequence, Earl made it a sport to bully Bobby in anyway he could get away with. Bobby withstood the heckling and browbeating to have the advantage that an older companion brought in resolving neighborhood conflicts. Besides, having learned from his father, he really didn't know any better alternative other than to endure the slaughter.

"Where you goin'?" Earl asked as the two walked out into the sunny part of the back yard.

"On vacation," Bobby mumbled as he gave a cheap, white plastic ball a not-so-successful kick.

"I know that, stupid," Earl said, eager to jump on the younger's lack of verbal comprehension. "Where you goin' on vacation?"

Bobby missed how he had been 'stupid' and answered more slowly. "Yosemite."

"My dad say's it's stupid to go on vacation to Yosemite. There's too many people."

Bobby advanced on the plastic ball and made a more successful whack at it, catching it solid on the point of his tennis shoe. "No it's not," he said in response to Earl's statement.

"Yes it is. It's stupid. Dad say's he's going to take us in the four wheel drive up to where nobody goes and we can do anything we want."

Bobby hung his head as he drew near to the ball and tapped at it repeatedly with the tip of his shoe. The round ball reminded him of a round wheel and a paradox presented itself to him. "We got four wheels on our car," he said in defense of his vacation.

"So," the older Earl blurted out trying to find an immediate hole in the logic. When nothing obvious was forthcoming, and indeed the logic seemed to stick, he continued, "So, you still can't go where we go. You can't." Then in a stroke of divergence that salvaged his ability to goad his companion he said, "You can't even leave the yard. Ha, ha. Little baby can't even leave the yard. Baby can't leave the yard; baby can't leave the yard; baby can't leave the yard...."

Bobby pulled his chin in to pout and glare. "Yes I can," he shouted against the progressing chant. "Yes I can."

"OK," Earl said, taunting him. "Prove it. Prove it little baby."

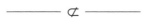

Senior Bob had worn his anger to near exhaustion. Forty-five dollars for a locksmith to come out to the lot, while he roasted, and make a plastic, temporary key. A stupid, stinking, filthy, damned, temporary key. For forty-five dollars! His hands were quaking from the rage. It would be five extra dollars to make it out of metal and Bob refused. Like a general rallying his defeated and retreating troops for a last stand, Generalissimo Roberto was going to lay down his life rather than surrender that last five bucks.

The young, Hispanic man doing the job was only one of a dozen or so technicians that worked for his company. He could sympathize with Bob, but was powerless to do anything about it. Forty-five dollars would lighten his wallet a bit too much also, but it was what the boss told him to charge so he did. The combination of emotions, sympathy and duty, presented themselves as a bland exterior of steadiness. "Well man," the young technician said, balancing his business with his morals, "that plastic key ain't gonna last long."

Bob took the sound advice as an attempt to juice him further. "Only cost two-damn-fifty at the hardware store."

The young man crossed the arms of his crisp, khaki locksmith uniform, and raised his dark, bushy eyebrows high. "Yeah, you can go there. But you gotta go right now because that ain't gonna last long."

"For forty-five dollars I should be able to get ten keys that last."

The young man took off his khaki hat and stared at the company logo while scratching his head. With any luck, he thought, one day he could own his own shop and pay others to take this crap. Replacing the cap he said, "If you don't need anything else, sir, I gotta get going. Thank-you for using Speedy Lock."

Bob just glared at the young man as he carefully pulled the company truck out of the lot. Thank-you indeed, thought Bob.

Before he had driven away, and before he had been filled up with Bob's vituperations, the young technician had told Bob all about opening locks and as to why this one had failed. The locksmith was well familiar with the tool Jeff had used to get the door open and knew all the problems it caused; one of which was a problem just like this. From the moment he heard this advice, Bob knew what he was going to do. He was going to march right over to Jeff's house and shove that bill in his face. Jeff was going to pay every penny of it.

Bob stewed the whole way home. Along the way, he added to the brewing mix of his attitude heat, traffic and fumes. When he pulled into the driveway he popped open the repaired door and stomped across the lawn to his neighbor's, red receipt in hand. His little chest heaved up and down, his lips stretched into a thin line. He jabbed the doorbell twice and, for good measure, banged on the door.

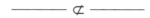

Sharon pulled her feet up under one side of her lap as she leaned over to get a tissue. She dabbed with both hands at the big, salty tears that were pooling under each eye, and then blew her nose. With both hands kneading the edge of the cloth couch, a tragic, un-requited love finished on the screen, lovers parting in the mist of a commencing train, the long, howling, mournful whistle lying over the top of their final dialogue.

"My sweet Loretta," the dashing partisan said to his beautiful paramour while standing on the entrance of the moving car, "I will never forget you. And the revolution will never forget what you have done."

Sharon snapped up another tissue and sniffed.

"I believe you my love," the brave heroine called, running beside the puffing, hissing train. "But, will there come a day when we will be able to forget the revolution?"

Music swelled, dripping honey sweet, and the housewife shut her eyes and felt the heroine's loss, her gain, and all the crazy emotions swirling around the confusion, death and triumph of the struggle. The door banged open and she was suddenly transported back to the three bedroom house in the suburbs. Standing in front of her was her husband, his shirt was off, and wadded up under his nose, portions of the white cloth saturated with blood. Both of his eyes were tearing and he had trouble navigating to his lounge chair.

Sharon stood up slapping a hand over her mouth. "What on earth happened to you?"

Bob slumped heavily in the lounge chair and bent it back until his head was parallel with the ground. "Ged me some ice," he groaned out.

Up the walkway, looking like a big worried puppy, Jeff came to the front door wringing his hands as if he were trying to crush walnuts between them. He stopped at the open door and called in. "It was an accident," he said apologetically. "I swear it was an accident."

"What was an accident?" a bewildered Sharon gasped out.

"Ged me some ice," groaned the bleeding man again.

Shaking his head Jeff explained, "It was a reflex. I opened the door; I had my head turned. And boom, somebody was right in my face with this red paper so, wham-o. I smack him."

Bob leaned up off the chair, lowering his t-shirt so that the blood spilled pitifully across his mouth as he talked. "You," he said through squinting, tearing eyes, managing to poke an index finger, "you ged oudda my house. Ged oudda here now."

"Bob, Bob," Sharon snapped excitedly, "you're bleeding all over your favorite chair. Put that shirt back over your nose."

"Ged me some ice, damn it. Ged me some ice and call da bolice."

Jeff put both hands out to the side, pleading. "It was an accident," he said. "I swear it was an accident."

From his prone position, "Ged oudda my house. Sharon, call da bolice."

Sharon looked back and forth between the two men totally flustered. "Bob," she said plaintively, "he said it was an accident. He said he was sorry."

The last sentence infuriated the bleeding man and he dropped the shirt one more time and rolled up onto an elbow. "Nebah," he said, spewing dribbles of blood, "he nebah said sorry. Nebah!"

"OK," yelled Jeff desperately, "I'm sorry. I'm really sorry."

Bob flopped back down. "Sharon. Sharon! Ged me some ice."

Sharon finally started toward the refrigerator. As she left the front room she exchanged a glance with the burly neighbor and they both shrugged their shoulders.

By this time, Jane, Jeff's wife, came striding up behind her husband, both arms wrapped tightly around her middle. She leaned into the room beside her big, burly and contrite spouse. "Is he alright?" she asked.

Sharon finally convinced Bob not to call the police. It was touch and go, however, after Jeff refused to pay for the locksmith. Sharon pleaded to his sense of fairness, in as much as Jeff was only trying to help. "And," she had offered, "just what would you do if someone jumped in your door shoving a paper in your face." This last statement was the clincher as Bob could not admit to the fact that he would not have punched an intruder barging into his house as the more macho Jeff had done. The police, with better things to do, stayed out it.

Cubes of ice, put in a plastic bag, behind a wet cloth, slowed the swelling and kept it from moving too far into each eye. The three of them, Jeff, Sharon and Jane, were pretty sure the nose was not broken and a doctor not called--this decided over the objections of the injured party. Since Bob could still keep his puffy eyes open well enough to drive he wanted to get going. And since he was injured, Sharon felt compelled not to argue the point.

"Wad time is id?" Bob asked from under the cold cloth.

"It's twelve-thirty. Time to get something to eat."

"Dwelve-dirdy," moaned Bob. "We godda ged going."

"Don't you want to eat first?"

"We'll go droo da drive-droo. We godda ged going."

"OK, if you feel good enough. Susan! Bobby! Let's get going."

Susan had managed a way around the injured spectacle straight to the car to un-pack her brand new mirror. After un-packing it, she decided it looked better in the package and meticulously reinserted the looking glass along with every piece of Styrofoam and plastic that had held it in place. When mom called she put the mirror up on the dresser, where it belonged, picked up her book and came into the front room. Dad was rising up off the lounger and removing the ice bag. Before Susan was a creature other than her father. The monster that had so callously smashed her mirror had now been transformed into looking like one. Blood still caked thick around the swollen nostrils. Puffy eyes gave him an oriental look, perhaps more chipmunk than oriental, perhaps a strange combination of the two. Purplish and green colors were already starting to striate the swelling and this final ghoulish tinge sent Susan back to clutching at her mother's skirt.

"Are you ready?" the monster asked, and Susan clung tighter.

Mom patted the back of her head. "Honey, are you ready?"

Not taking her eyes off of her transmogrified father, whose voice had transformed with the features, she shook her head up and down.

"Where's your brother?" mom asked.

Susan just shook her head again, staring.

"Where's your brudda?" the big ogre repeated, and Susan retreated behind the skirt altogether, only leaving the top of her head showing to continue the gaze.

Bob turned to his wife. "Well?" he asked. "Where's Bobby?"

Down the old alley way, transformed into a battle line by Earl's imagination, the two boys fought their way from garbage can to garbage can, and from telephone pole to telephone pole, staying hot on the heels of the retreating enemy firing their super-secret finger guns the whole way. Bombs exploded in air as signified by handfuls of dirt launched skyward. Grenades in the disguise of rocks were sent in retaliation after the pin was removed from clinched teeth. Machine gun fire peppered the aluminum garbage cans when a side-arm sling of gravel met it square. Earl had been wounded several times and continued to become injured each and very time Bobby achieved an equal number of impairments. But the advance continued.

At the end of the alley, where the more imaginative dirt and gravel became plain old cement and asphalt, the two boys scampered for cover behind a car parked parallel to the street. Little Bobby looked back down the long alley-way. Remembering that the original objective of the war had been to drive the enemy down to the end, he decided to celebrate a hard won victory.

"Yippee," the five year old squealed jumping up and down, throwing his hands up, "we won, we won."

Earl could not believe how imprudent his young private was being. Only a ten star general like himself could decide when the enemy was actually vanquished. "Get down, get down," yelled Earl and jumped from his crouched position to knock the foolish private to the ground. "They're still there."

From under the larger boy, Bobby looked across the street. "Where?" he whispered.

"Down there," Earl whispered back. "Down that next alley. Keep me covered and I'll go first."

As Earl got up and prepared for his death-defying Sprint into hostile territory, Bobby looked back down the long alley. It had surely grown much longer since he came down it. Somewhere near the vanishing point was his house. It must be at least a hundred miles back home, he thought.

"Hey," Earl chided the recruit, wondering if he should bust him to buck-private for not paying attention, "cover me."

Bobby looked down the elongating corridor one more time, bit his lip, and then said, "OK, you're covered."

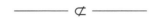

Senior Bob was physically better now that the swelling had gone down a little and his voice returned to normal. But his stomach was in knots and his little intestines braided into a sort of finely tethered macramé' set and could absolutely not be un-tie-able under present conditions. "Of course I don't want any lunch," he snapped at his wife, who was still attempting to dote over her injured spouse. "How can I get any food down my throat when I can barely breathe?" After all the enterprise, the planning, the straining, the contorting to get these people off their butt and on the road, just when the time was eminent, just when his wife had agreed to the move and stop opposing him, little Bobby had disappeared.

"You need to relax honey," his wife told him in a breathy, whiny way that only added fuel to the machine that was forcing up his blood pressure. "Your face is all red and everything."

"Well it ain't purple yet," he snapped, voice hoarse from screeching his child's name, and started out the door again in search of his errant son.

Jeff was still repentant enough about smacking his neighbor in the schnoz to aide in the search. By now it was two o'clock and the heat of the day was nearing its zenith. The sidewalk, nearly white, reflected the sun up to blind the eyes. When crossing streets waves of heat powered out of the energy reservoir of the black asphalt baking everything from the bottom up with an intensity greater than the object which had poured energy into it in the first place. Sweat stung the eyes. Thoughts grew muddled and un-focused. And poor Bob senior, hungry, dehydrated, and livid, felt as if he was going to collapse.

The search would have been much more effective had it been coordinated. Jeff would cross one intersection moments before Bob came along. Bob wandered down streets Jeff had just turned off of. Streets were left uncovered, alleys bypassed. Sharon, who was supposed to be manning the phones, spent the whole time talking to the lady down the block who had just started flying lessons--Sharon had always wanted to take flying lessons.

Bob stood in the middle of one intersection feeling the heat bake right through his tennis shoes. He squint his eyes in all four directions and licked his dry lips. Nothing. He looked at his watch and swooned. It was almost three. It was time to take serious action, he thought. He would use the car for speed and knock on the door of every person he had ever had even a passing conversation with. Hell, he thought as addled thoughts tripped over waves of heat, I'll put up posters if I have to. I'll call all the radio stations and pay them to broadcast a plea. I'll rent a damn plane and fly it with a banner trailing behind it saying

'Bobby, go home or die.' "This is it," he gasped out loud, smacking the fleshy part of his fist into the other hand, "this is war." He didn't know how right he was.

Sharon stretched the cord of the phone to the front window, pulled back the curtain and watched as her husband pulled away from the house. "It's Bob," she said to her flying friend. "I wonder where he's going? Anyway, what was the difference between flaps and ailerons again?"

The steering wheel was too hot to hold, but Bob squeezed it tight. The pain from it, somehow, made him feel as if he were accomplishing something. The dark blue, vinyl seat roasted his back side and back as surely as if he were suspended over a broiler. Not near enough wind came in the window and when he turned on the fan the only air that came to him had been super-heated by the grilling dash-board. In a final attempt at some sort of relief, he leaned out the window. But when the soft, under part of his arm met the sizzling blue paint he howled and pulled back inside.

"Damnit," he yelled. "By damn it I'm going to find that kid and rattle his teeth loose."

Not three blocks away, in an alley that had been overlooked on the first two sweeps; a much calmer Jeff had finally spied the two rascals rolling around inside a garbage can which was serving their purpose as a tank. Jeff scolded his son a little and told Bobby how upset his dad was. By and large, however, he was in good spirits. Or, rather, the good spirits were in him. Jeff had been searching while drinking ice cold beer, periodically rubbing the cold can around his face, only stopping the reconnaissance when supplies got low. In an hour of searching, Jeff had gone from nearly empty to tanked.

"Oh my," Sharon commented into the phone, "there they are."

She had seen them coming up the walk through the curtain. "I better go good luck with the flying."

Sharon ran to the door and pulled it open. A pleasantly smiling Jeff had Bobby on his thick shoulders. Earl was already home. Jeff's face was red and drops of sweat saturated the surface. The t-shirt could have been freshly retrieved from a swimming pool, his hairy belly showing through the thin, soaked cloth.

"Here they are," he said, clumsily lowering Bobby to the ground, wobbling a little.

Sharon squatted down until she met her son eye to eye. "Young man," she said in that voice only a mother possesses the voice that still can raise the hackles of grown men who are prone to flashing back to their childhood, "I am very, very angry with you. Go to your room and I will be in shortly and we will talk about this."

Jeff had brushed by mother and child and moved right into the kitchen. Sharon watched her son go down the hall with the shadow of foreboding following him, and then noticed Jeff. It was unusual for him to come in even when invited, so Sharon was more surprised to see him perusing her refrigerator.

"Has he got any beer in here?" Jeff asked, leaning heavily on the open door.

Sharon came into the kitchen and puzzled over the large man's behavior, all of him hidden behind the open refrigerator save his backside and hairy arm. Jeff looked up over the top of the white, enameled door and gave Sharon a strange look. A look she interpreted as confused or in pain.

"Goddamn that feels good," he groaned and let out a big sigh.

As his big head and curly black hair lowered again out of sight, Sharon's imagination ran wild. "What feels good?" she asked suspiciously and took a precautionary step backward

"The cold air," Jeff said and Sharon could hear him rummaging. "Ah, here we go." Jeff stood up holding a can of Bob's beer and slammed the door. As he opened the can he said, "Damn, it's so hot out there. Bake your scalp right off your head. And I mean clear off. Feels like there ain't nothin' left but old, dry bones up there right now."

Sharon deciphered the situation as Jeff cocked back his head to drain half the can. "So, I see you've had a few?" Sharon said while crossing her arms.

The big man thought about it for a few seconds, then stuck out his lower lip, closed his eyes and shrugged his shoulders. He offered one hand, palm up in resignation. He tried to respond but only succeeded in blowing a few short busts of air over his drooping lip. When no thoughts came to him, and he had forgotten the question anyway, he tilted back the can to finish it, popped open the door and helped himself to another.

"Jeff?"

"Mmmm-hmmmmmmmm," the prolonged humm came out.

"Why don't you have a seat and I'll give Jane a call. How about that?"

Jeff closed the door again, this time with exaggerated care, wobbling the whole time. He shrugged his shoulders again, smacked his lips around a while and said, "Sure, sure, whatever is protocol."

He opened his beer and continued his talking while he made his way into the front room and into Bob's favorite lounge chair. "What you guys got in this house? A swamp cooler? Same as us. Swamp coolers ain't worth a shit..." Jeff plopped a meaty hand over his mouth as he leaned back all the way in the lounger. "Oops, I'm sorry. Shouldn't talk like that in somebody's house. Course I talk like that in my house. Jane, she don't even try no more. She thinks Earl is gonna pick it up." He wafted a thick, hairy hand in the air to help dispel this silly notion from his wife. "But, hell, he hears worse shit than that out on the play-yard every day."

"That's fine," Sharon said condescendingly while dialing the phone. "Just fine."

Jeff scratched the side of his noggin, making a grating sound akin to two pieces of wood rubbing together. "That ain't fine," he said with an embellished facial contortion to the negative. "That ain't fine at all."

"Busy, busy, busy," Bob yelled, getting progressively louder and more enraged with each word. "Every time I call she's on the damn phone. Blab, blab, blab, blab, blab!" With the last word he smacked the receiver down on the hook. The phone was becoming his enemy. Six times he had called and six times it had been nothing but that infuriating beep, beep, beep, and beep. Sharon had not wanted to get 'call waiting.' She had said, "I just hate being interrupted." Bob stared at the boxy pay phone and twisted up his face to spew out in a venomous, mocking tone, "I just hate being interrupted." Bob could feel his knees quaking. If he had been in the desert, vultures would have started circling. He was so dry that sweat barely was coming out of him. "I'll find that kid," he rasped out, shaking a fist in the air. "I'll find him if it takes years."

Sharon let the phone ring almost twenty times. She stretched the cord until she could peak out the side window and look at Jeff's driveway. There she saw Jane start up the Bronco. Earl was in the seat beside her.

"Oh darn," she whispered, hung up the phone, and ran for the door. It was too late.

She exited the house just in time to see the big, four wheel drive round the curve in the road. She stood in the driveway, tapping her foot, wondering what to do. In all her experience in handling household affairs with aplomb, there was no precedent for removing an unwanted, drunken houseguest. When all polite options faded, she became resolute. "I've just got to throw him out. Just like that. Can't have him in there all drunk like that."

By the time she re-entered to tell her unwanted house guest to get out the door, she found Jeff snoring gently with his last beer balanced on his sizable belly. The beer undulated gently with the rhythm of each breath. Sharon crossed her arms and blew an irritated puff out through her cheeks. Being rude to a houseguest did not come easily to Sharon, even an uninvited and drunk one. She pulled the beer can out of his slumbering hand and gave him a little, apprehensive shake on the shoulder. "Jeff," she said, quietly at first, then louder and louder. "Jeff, Jeff, Jeff."

She stamped her foot and punched the man on the shoulder. "Hey," she yelled, then set down the beer and started clapping her hands by his ear. "Hey, Jeff." Nothing.

Since there were no results from the conventional, Sharon felt like taking drastic measures. Bob would just go nuts if she didn't get him out of the house. Her mind wandered. She then remembered her movie and how the handsome partisan had shaken the drunken Paco out of his stupor. She went into the kitchen, grabbed a dish towel, and filled a glass of water to the brim. Just before the front room she surveyed the amount of liquid in the glass. Fearing that it was a little too excessive, she poured half of it back into the sink and went to the chair with only half a glass.

She raised the glass high in one hand, having the towel ready with the other. When he came to, she reasoned, she would hand him the towel to keep him from being angry. She started the downward stroke of her arm and caught herself. "Come on," she said to herself out loud gathering courage, "it's not going to hurt him or anything. It didn't hurt Paco." She knew that splashing water into someone's face wasn't actually anything to be afraid of. It was just that it seemed harsh and so impolite. All he was doing was sleeping. He, after all, had found the boys. But he was drunk. Drunk and sleeping in her husband's favorite chair. She steeled herself, raised the glass again, and fired the contents straight into his face. Nothing.

The big man snorted a few times, smacked his lips, and continued snoring. After all the tension of the build-up to the splash-down, it was quite deflating. Sharon let her arms droop and said, "Oh great. Just what am I supposed...?" She looked up and in the hall witnessing the scene was Susan. "Young lady," Sharon yapped out in embarrassment, "what are you looking at?" Susan retreated down the hall. Sharon felt her face flush red and flapped her arms against her side. "Oh great. Now really great."

Bob was a beaten man. A foot soldier of the Africa Corps trudging the thousand miles of desert from El Alamein to an uncertain fate. Lawrence without a camel, walking the dunes, trying desperately to stave off dehydration just so the British could shoot him like a dog. Hopeless. His scalp baked. His mouth was thick and dry. The car crept like the wounded soldier he imagined himself to be.

Vacation was ruined. His plans of leaving today battered by the high velocity shells of inertia. The sedan limped into its parking spot as if crawling onto its final funeral pyre. Bob let his head droop and then looked to the house. "Call the police," he said dramatically and miserably. "Must call the police. Bobby's probably been stolen by some pervert and I can't do anything to save him."

The truth be known, Bob knew Bobby was most probably out on a lark and not in any danger at all. He was trying to balance his seething anger with parental worry only to minimize the impact when he finally did see his nappy headed scion appear from some aimless wondering. The parental worry also settled nicely with his gloomy, over-wrought sense of failure at not getting his own way at the start of what should have been a very relaxing time.

The bone-weary, vanquished soldier stopped at the oasis in form of a hose and let it run until the water was cool, as cool as the pool of a harem's master. He removed his foreign legion's chapeau and let the water pour over his head and greedily down the throat. He heard the door rattle and was back in the suburb with his plain wife giving him a most un-romantic stare.

"Now don't be too angry," Sharon said in a hoarse whisper, pulling the door to behind her.

Parental worry took the back exit out of Bob's brain as anger chased it with a crow bar. "Bobby's back. Isn't he?"

Sharon puzzled at the direction of her husband's anger. As far as she was concerned the news of little Bobby's return was long ago. She had been apologizing for Jeff.

"And you," snapped the red-faced spouse, Adam's apple giggling up and down.

"Me?" questioned Sharon extra puzzled, hand flat against a beguileless chest.

"Yes you. Talking on the phone all damn day. Blab, blab, blab, blab." Then in his mocking nasal. "You hate interruptions. No call waiting. I've been looking all over damn town...."

"Quiet," Sharon demanded, "the neighbors will hear." Then she caught herself. The only neighbor in ear shot was out of reach of any earthly voice.

Thinking of the one, fat, arrogant neighbor whom he blamed for all his present trouble--all the trouble, that is, he didn't presently blame on his wife--Bob became incensed. He started jumping up and down screaming, "Neighbors, neighbors, neighbors, neighbors...."

Sharon watched her red-faced husband doing his silly dance and got angry herself. She stalked into the house, slammed the door and locked it, along with the dead bolt, and put on the safety chain. She stamped her foot and snorted at the adolescence of her thirty-five year old husband. She crossed her arms, spun as she started off in a brisk walk and nearly fell over the top of Jeff's, prone, wreaking, catatonic corpse. Just what the hell was she going to say about this?

"Dad's gonna whup your butt," Susan said to her precocious sibling. He had been acting much too comfortable and relaxed and Susan took it upon herself to remind him of the predicament he was in. "When he gets home he's gonna whup it good."

Bobby stopped his mid-bed rollicking and frowned at his sister. He didn't like to be reminded of facts when he was in trouble. Leave it to his sister to do such a thing. But Bobby knew where the control lie, who would do the punishment and to what factors the severity of the 'whupping' would be attached to. Antagonizing his sister would not increase his punishment an iota. Little Bobby picked up a pillow on the bed and launched it at his sister, then lunged for the end where she was lying and tried to grab her book.

Susan ducked the pillow and easily wrestled the book out of the arms of her younger brother. "Get away," she commanded and got up to move out of her brother's territory. "Dad's gonna whup your butt," she said again and slammed the door hard just as Bobby picked up his super-soaker.

Proud and unyielding the swaggering cowboy stared at the outside of the door expecting it to pop open under the stern glare. After a while, a not-so proud and a just-a-little yielding cowboy continued the vigil. In a few more seconds, plain old Bob was tapping sheepishly on the door.

When no answer came, Bob did what he usually did when locked out of the house; he went to plead his case at the window. The usual window of pleading, on the porch, was covered completely with the inner shade. As a consequence, he went off the porch and worked his way carefully between the large, thorny rosebushes to the front room window. The drapes were pulled back. He scanned the empty front room until he came to a pair of socks. The socks were sweaty, dirty, and full of feet, sticking up off the end of his favorite chair. Behind the feet there was the arc of a huge belly, heaving up and down with each breath. The belly belonged to Jeff.

Bob was aghast. He felt what was left of his manly pride drain into his shoes; gush up over his socks and out the eyelets of the laces. Ridiculous yet powerful thoughts of infidelity pulsed through his over-heated brain. As reason tried to prevail, the pernicious side of him poured on the heat with all sorts of questions. Why was there a man sleeping in his favorite chair? Was this the reason she had locked him out? Maybe this is why she doesn't like being interrupted. It was ridiculous, of course, but being ridiculous was never a deterrent to Bob.

Seeing that the window was unlatched, Bob clutched at the little aluminum screen that covered the old window and yanked it out of its place by kinking the flimsy frame beyond its prescribed flexibility. He then clawed at the bottom of the old, wood-paned window and worked it slowly open. The old frame was heavy and no longer cantilevered. It wedged into an open position delicately.

The jealous husband was going to sneak in and spring like a coiled snake. He was going to front down the icy harlot that had defiled his bed and sow shame wherever it might grow. He leaned his vengeful head slowly into the room just as a snake might slither stealthily to its prey.

Just then, translated along the walls, through the floor and ceiling was the vibration of a slammed door. A door slammed in complete innocence by Susan only to escape a snotty little brother. The vibration rattled the old window, with its heavy, lead counter weights lying somewhere in dirty walls of the foundation, and broke it loose. The head of the snake would never be the same.

Bob felt his eyes blow out of his head and mix with an eternity of multi-colored stars, only to resettle back in the sockets as crossed as any maiden-form bra might wish to be. The explosion had been two fold as one moving down from the back of his head as the sash smacked him, and another moving from the chin upward as it met the solid sill. Bob's head was locked inside the room looking like it had been mounted, mounted in a position well below proper viewing.

The groggy man, nearly senseless, or at least more senseless than before, began yanking back against the trap, stretching his neck with strained groans. Sharon, from the bedroom where she had been sulking by watching another soap-opera, heard the gurgles and grunts and ran toward the front room. She was anxious and repulsed as she thought the noise was coming from a retching Jeff. Along the way, she scooped up the bathroom waste basket anticipating a fountain of vomitus.

Coming around the corner, she puzzled over the slumbering, intoxicated man. He still had a silly grin spread across his ample red face and was snoring contentedly. But the grunts and straining continued.

Sharon moved her stereoscopic hearing back and forth, zooming in on the direction of the sounds. She turned slowly and saw her husband's head jutting out from the base of the window like some latter-day, suburban gargoyle.

"Bob, is that you?" Sharon questioned, half expecting a negative answer. "Bob," she said again louder, "what are you doing?" The pieces of the puzzle came to the perplexed wife only after some musing. At first she thought he was playing some sort of childish game--with the silly look on his face and all. Even after the events lined up in correct order she didn't realize the severity of the situation. Finally figuring out he was trapped, she decided to lift the sash.

The muddled Bob was convinced something was pinching him in two. Some mechanical vice had gone haywire and was trying to tweak his head right off. It was of the utmost importance to get out from between those pinchers or he would be finished. When mild struggle hadn't freed him, Bob placed both hands against the sill, feet against the foundation, and gave a furious pull just in time to have Sharon liberate the addled head.

Much to Sharon's dismay, Bob was rocket propelled in reverse. With a defiant yell, her husband lunged backward with all his might to pierce into the exact middle of the large, thorny rosebushes. Now a noise of a different sort came out of Bob.

If it had been louder and with more gusto one could have called the sounds emanating from the middle of the large, thorny rose bush a screech. But Bob wasn't up to screeching and what came out sounded more like a long, prolonged, audible gasp.

"Aaaaaaaaaah," Bob went in agony as he imagined himself inside a ball of barbed wire. "Aaaaaaaaaaah."

Sharon, who was still holding the garbage can, sprints out the front door to the bushes which were cradling her husband. All she could see of her dearly beloved was one hand sticking out the top of the tight green mass, and a foot jutting horizontal out one side. "Bob?" she asked again. "Bob? Are you all right?"

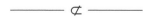

Sharon extricated her poor, miserable husband with the care of a surgeon, though not the expertise. Back and forth the two bickered and kibitzed over the most efficacious strategy. One argued from the opinion of perspective, the other from sheer passion of entanglement. "This branch first." "No, that branch." "This one?" "Don't move that one it hurts." "This one?" "DON'T TOUCH IT!" On and on Sharon proceeded; thorn by thorn, branch by branch, clippers in hand, until her husband was freed and the two formerly proud rose bushes resembled an old, worn out, raffia- weave party hat that had visited way too many college keggers.

The children had come out and were more than willing to get in on the kibitzing. Dad's groaning both scared and excited them. When the fear gave way to the excitement of the extraction, both Bobby and Susan fed mom suggestions a mile a minute. "Get it wet, that'll make it soft," Bobby suggested. "Cut down low and we can save the flowers," Susan opined. When both mom and dad tired of such banter and they were dispatched, they went to the neighbor's oleander bush and took turns jumping into the middle and getting each other out in a most efficient manner--in methods obviously superior to the job mom was doing.

Bob sat slumped into Sharon's vanity with an ice pack on the back of his neck to abate his throbbing head. Sharon was dabbling iodine liberally onto every red scratch on her husband's soft white body. When she was through there were reddish blobs over substantial portions of his blanched carcass. From a distance he looked polka-dotted or as if he was suffering from the worst case of measles in modern medical literature. Coupled with the greenish-purple which surrounded his eyes he looked like he might have stepped out of a flying saucer. Sharon chatted as she dabbed on the staining goo.

"Oh Bobby," she teased, "You were jealous. You were jealous. How long has it been since you were jealous?" The idea of her husband's jealousy had started out ridiculous and insulting. But now, nursing him back to health under her care, the idea seemed mildly captivating.

Bob rose up his chin with a pouting expression and craned his neck to look at his wife. "Just what the hell was I supposed to think?"

Sharon gave him a patronizing smile and said, "You just might think that some fat drunk fell asleep in your chair." Then, just because it added to the color scheme, she took the cotton swab and splattered a dab of iodine on the end of his gawking beak.

"Quit," snapped Bob wafting a hand too late in defense of his beezer.

The two children were on the bed, lying on their stomachs, propping their heads up with their elbows and watching the resuscitation of their father with keen interest. For both of them this was better than Halloween. First of all dad never got dressed for Halloween and, secondly, he was a lot scarier than anything they had seen to date.

Little Bobby was listening to his mother's teasing and turned to sister for advice. "What's jealous?" he asked. He was half sure, but wanted to get the other half nailed down.

Susan answered quickly and confidently. "It means you want something I ain't got," she said.

Sharon scratched her head and smiled. The mis-definition went right by Bob and he followed up. "Well, I'll tell you what I want that I ain't got," he said miserably. "I want to be in our campsite cooking up some trout. Our whole vacation is all screwed up. Might as well not even go now."

"Oh Bob," Sharon said, much nicer than if the statement had occurred an hour ago, "we can still get going. There's plenty of light. We've got a whole week."

"No we can't. It's ruined. They'll give our reservations to someone else. Might as well just stay home."

Sharon was intrigued by the sudden role reversal and put her mighty will into it. "Kids," she commanded, "get your things and get out to the car. Right now."

"Aw, Sharon, it's too late."

"Here's your shirt. Everything's ready. Let's go."

"It's too late."

"I'll see you in the car."

Bob stood up to put on his shirt watching his wife walk down the hall. Maybe this was finally a go. Maybe they were finally going to get on the road. Who cares if it's too late for today? It sure would get tomorrow off to an early start. Sure. What the heck? Might as well take what life gives you and get on with it. Bob planted his hat, fussily orientated it, and marched toward the front door.

When he entered the front room, he saw his wife standing still and staring. He moved forward to stare also. There they stood, both of them watching the quiet, peaceful undulations of the huge belly of the sleeping man.

"Did you try ice water?" Bob asked, wanting instead to pour a bucket of scalding steam.

"No, just tap water. Let me try again."

The two kids had marched right past the slumbering drunk straight for the car as if leaving a passed out man in their front room might be a very normal thing to do while going on vacation. Sharon brought another glass of water, this one from the jug in the refrigerator. Bob eagerly took it from her and, without hesitation, smacked it into Jeff's face with some velocity: Less than nothing. Where before Jeff had bothered to stir and smack his lips, this time he merely coughed out what water had entered his open mouth in one, large convulsion and continued his pleasant snoring.

"I knew it was too good to be true," Bob said. "What do we do now?"

Sharon looked at her husband whose blood pressure was starting to rise again. Since she had made up her mind to go, she was going to go now regardless of anything. It is a strange thing this perception of capability. One hour ago all circumstances would have been insurmountable to walking out the front door. Now, because of a shift in judgment, nothing would deter her. "Well," she said as resolute as when her daughter had defined jealousy, "I know exactly what we're going to do."

The door clicked shut with a note pinned to the slumbering man's chest, reading: Jeff, please lock the door when you leave. Sorry about all the water, will explain when we get home.

Bob, wounded as he was, felt his whole spirit pick up finally being on the road. Even though he was not yet out of town, he felt as if the adventure was already beginning. Every joint began the slow process of loosening up. Internal organs started to function properly without the tight string of stress around them. In fact, Bob became so relaxed so quickly he became very drowsy and stopped at a drive-through to get a big cup of coffee.

Just before the freeway, on the side of one of those horrible expressways with the cement curb for a median that won't let you do anything but drive straight forever, Bob swung the old sedan into the fast food joint. He followed the signs around to the back where they led to the landscaped and curbed trough that funneled cars past the window. There was one car in front of him at the order intercom.

The heat while the car was moving was bearable, but when they were stopped it was horrible. And they waited. And waited. The car in front of them was taking an extremely long time. Bob tapped at the heat gauge to make sure it was telling him the truth. The car was getting ready to over-heat, spewing its excess out the bottom due to the fan, and into the passenger compartment. Bob had already decided to back out of the chute and go into the nice, air-conditioned eatery when the car in front finally moved.

"Hello," cackled the little speaker in the big, plastic menu board, "welcome to Fatso's Burger Basket. May I help you?"

"Yeah," said Bob, "I'd like a...."

"I wanna soda," yelled Bobby.

"I want one too," yelled Susan.

"What?" cackled the box.

"Oh Bob," Sharon said, "Get me something to drink too."

Bob leaned to the box again. "I said I want a...."

Since his request had not been specifically acknowledged, Bobby yelled again, "I wanna soda."

"What?" the box rasped again.

"I'll get you a soda. Now be quiet."

"I want one too," chimed in Susan.

"I'll get you one too."

"What?"

"Three small cokes and one large coffee."

"I have an order for three small cokes and one large coffee. Will that be all sir?"

"Make mine a large," Sharon said.

"I wanna a large too," yelled Bobby.

"Me too," Susan chimed in.

"You kids only need a small," Bob said craning his neck toward the back seat. Then back toward the box, "Make that one more large Coke."

"OK, I have an order for three small cokes, one large coke and a large coffee. Will that be all?"

"No, I want two small cokes, one large coke and one large coffee."

Bobby undid his safety belt and pulled himself up to his feet by using dad's headrest. Leaning close to the driver's side window and right by his father's ear Bobby yelled to the intercom, "Two large Cokes."

"Bobby," commanded dad, "get down."

"So, I have an order for two small cokes, two large cokes and one large coffee."

"No, no," Bob snapped, hot and disgusted, "I want three small cokes, and one large coffee."

"Bob," Sharon whimpered, "I want a large coke."

"OK, so I have an order for three small cokes and one large coffee."

"No, no, no, I want three small cokes... I mean, I want two small cokes and one large coke and...."

"A large coke," Bobby yelled again.

Dad swung clear around this time to give his son the evil eye. "You're having a small," dad confirmed. "Now sit down."

"Yes Bobby," mom conferred, "sit down. You only need a small."

"What about me mom?" Susan asked.

"Alright. So I have an order for two small cokes and two large cokes."

"No, no, no," Bob roared, "I want three small cokes and one large coke and one large coffee."

"OK. An order for...."

"I mean two small cokes and one large."

"Sir?"

"Yes?"

"Are drinks the only thing you want?"

"Yeah."

"Why don't you just pull up to the window and we'll get your order there?"

Bob was instantly indignant. "Why?" he demanded. "Why do I have to get my order at the window when everybody else can get it from here?"

"I think it'll just be easier, sir."

"From the length of time it took to get that last guy through here I don't think you people do anything the easy way. I'll just get my drinks somewhere else. And don't think that I'm ever going to come back, either."

"Bob," Sharon said reaching out to pat her husband's arm, "it's nothing to get so upset about."

"Yeah, well I know when I'm being talked down to." He turned from his wife to the box. "And I'm never going to come back here again as long as I live."

Irate Bob shifted the column into reverse and put his right arm up on the bench seat to turn around. As he swung his head around him saw the line of three cars waiting patiently behind him. Bob felt like he was in a hamster tube.

Bob waived for the car behind to back up. The man in the car behind looked behind him and responded by tapping on the horn and raising both hands in a "what the hell do you want?" gesture.

"Bob," Sharon said, "it'll be alright. I'll order for us." Sharon leaned over the top of her sweating husband to the window. "Hello," she said. "Hello, I would like to order some drinks." After a small pause she sat back down. "I don't think they're listening to us anymore."

Bob shifted back into drive. "Well, I'm going to just drive right past that window and don't be surprised if I let them know how I feel when I do."

Dad roared past the sign and around the corner that lined them up with the delivery window. Sitting in front of the window was the same car that had taken so long ordering. He gripped the steering wheel hard enough to make his knuckles white. After a few minutes he even honked his horn.

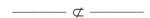

Work was not exactly Maria's raison d'être. Two semesters short of her bachelors in Biology Maria rightfully had better things to worry about than how to be the premier assistant manager for a Fasto's Burger Basket. But she tried to do the best job she could. For not investing her ego in the position, and keeping things in proper perspective, Maria was by far the favorite manager among the lower employees. Most of them were also undergraduates from the local university and shared the idea that there was a bigger, brighter world outside of Fatso's. They could always count on Maria to be fair, objective and, above all, knowing there should be larger worries in life beyond assembling hamburgers--a fact which seemed to elude most of the other managers.

Saturdays were always hectic and this one was no exception. People seemed to want to take out their stress from the week on any poor slob who had to work on a weekend. Far short of being compassionate, people seemed to disdain workers on minimum wage. Maria would remember this fact someday when she was a highly paid bio-engineer. But for now it was just "smile and take it" to all the assholes who didn't have anything better to do with their miserable lives than yell at an employee of Fatso's Burger Basket.

The honking horn brought her out of the back room where she was doing inventory and collecting supplies. They were short on sesame seed buns and the biology undergraduate was having to bicker with a supplier with a High School GED certificate who insisted on lecturing her in the fine art of tabulating burger buns. She could tell by the way the staff was milling around exchanging glances that there was a problem customer on the way to the drive-up window.

"What's the problem Dorothy?" she asked the young lady with the headset.

Dorothy, a plump African-American girl with pressed hair, looked embarrassed and tried to explain. "I couldn't get this guy's order and I told him to go ahead and come to the window. It really pissed him off, I guess."

Maria flicked her head toward the car waiting behind the little sliding window. "Is that him?" she asked.

"No. The next guy."

Just then the horn blared again and giggles reverberated around the work place. Maria opened the window and told the driver waiting it would just be a second. The driver shrugged his shoulders, jabbed a thumb towards Bob and company and shook his head in dismay. "I ain't in any hurry," he said.

Dorothy handed the large order to the man waiting at the window. Maria gave the poor, young clerk a break and told her she would take care of the disgruntled customer. Dorothy was grateful and stood back from the window. Just before the man drove off, the horn honked one more time and another round of chuckling rumbled through the eatery.

Though she sympathized, she could have none of it. Any kind of sniggering would only send an unsatisfied customer into a fit. She faced the toiling, busy workers and gave an announcement. "Alright, you guys, let's please have it quiet."

Behind her, she could feel the car move into place. With a deep breath, and a small prayer of patience, she turned and opened the window. What greeted her shocked her out of her regular demeanor.

Leaning toward the window was a gawking, long nosed, gargoyle with orange polka-dots and purple-green eyes. The gargoyle, replete with an orange dot tipping its beak, bared its teeth and gave a gurgle, meant to be a growl. Maria could feel herself losing control. As the gargoyle spoke she bit her lip. Then had to clasp her hand over her mouth.

"If we weren't so hot and thirsty," the angry customer spit out, "waiting forever in this stupid line, we'd go somewhere else. But I guess you've got us over a barrel this time. And furthermore..."

Maria's whole body began to quiver. She tried to get out the standard apology and, instead, let out a snicker. That one, guttural snigger from the boss let out an avalanche of tense laughter from the employees who were all witnessing the odd specter at the drive-up window. Maria could feel a hot sweat coming on as she fought to keep under control.

In a maniacal, wild-eyed shriek, the customer leaned out the window, his grotesque countenance twisting on his tawny neck, and yelled, "What the hell you laughing at?"

The purple, bloodshot and bulging eyes were the last straw. Maria put her head into both hands and let loose with a raucous laugh. She squat down behind the window, horrified at her insolence toward a customer, but unable to control it. He was just so goofy looking. She stayed below the window, balanced on a knife edge of chagrin and embarrassment yet in convulsive laughter. To her relief, she heard the car pull away. She peeked up over the railing to make sure it was true. When she turned to face her workers they gave her a cheer. To them she had been a hero, but Maria felt like crying.

"I won't take that crap. I won't take that from anybody. I'm going to sue. I'm going to write the owner of the company. That little, giggling girl is going to lose her job if it's the last thing I do." Bob was fuming, fretting and spitting out his words with all the venom he could muster.

The car jerked back and forth with his oral emphasis and Sharon chided him. "Bob," she whined, "you're driving like a mad-man. Calm down. It's nothing to get so upset over."

Bob jerked the car to a halt at the stop-light and glared at his wife. "Nothing to get mad at? Maybe you weren't in the car a few minutes ago?"

Sharon stared back at her seething husband; eyes raccooned in the garish make-up of bruising tissue, face dabbled here and there with orange iodine, and suddenly saw what the poor young woman in the window had found so humorous. She let out a little giggle and said, "Well, you do look kind of funny."

Little Bobby concurred loudly from the back seat. "Yeah dad, you look funny." Bob spun around and gave his son a look that wasn't funny at all. Susan, who was slow with her own glare, stopped grinning.

"Oh Bob," Sharon said, "Stop being such a pill. Now let's get something to drink. I'm parched."

The old sedan continue to rumble down the expressway with no where to turn. On the other side of the road there came another fast food joint. Bob gritted his teeth as they made their way past it. Not being able to cut across the divider and go directly to the eatery wasn't just inconvenient to the angry mottled-white male; it was an infringement upon his basic rights. This was silly, he thought. Some arrogant, fat-cat, bureaucrat with nothing better to do thought up some way to inconvenience good people and spend more money.

Up ahead was the entrance to the freeway. Somehow, to the affronted mottled-white male, this marked a metaphorical boundary to the beginning of his vacation. Once past the entry ramp on this pathetic expressway there could be no return to it. Once upon the freeway there could be no getting off of it. Bob, in his mind, needed to make a stand. There was a traffic light directly in front of the on ramp. Cross traffic exited the freeway from left to right. The entry was just on the other side of the intersection. Bob, with a shot of adrenalin, took his stand for family, country, freedom and the American way and turned on his left turn signal.

"Bob," Sharon complained, "it says you can't turn left."

Indeed, on the light pole there was a sign with an arrow veering left and a red circle with a slash through it superimposed. Bob leaned up tight to the steering wheel and pretended not to hear his wife. He was going to show those idiot bureaucrats. He was going to beat back the tyranny of the expressway and get his family something to drink before they died of thirst.

"Bob," Sharon mewled in a long sing-song whine. "You can't turn here."

"We'll see who can't do what."

"But Bob…"

The light turned green and before the opposing traffic could make their way across the intersection the old sedan squealed its tires in a cloud of blue smoke and roared around in a U-turn back toward the fast food joint.

Father Bob was triumphant. "Just show's you that you can do a lot more in life than you think," he crowed to his wife.

It had been a long time since he had seen such audacity. In the pummeling heat, which made him curse the broken air-conditioner and grow apathetic to duty, he was almost inclined to reward the audacious idiot by letting him go. Yet, Officer Johnson was surrounded by good tax-paying citizens who had, along with him, witnessed the hair-brained maneuver. He reached down and flipped on the lights.

Bob's face was red enough to almost blot out the iodine dots; and he did blend nicely with the flashing lights. He took the ticket without a word, keeping himself bottled up. He felt as if he had let one word out he would have gone off like an untied balloon and spurt around backward until he landed in jail. Tyranny, he thought to himself over and over, nothing but tyranny. Sharon instinctively knew that it was time to keep the "I told you so" under wraps. Besides, the stupidity of the ticket would make for a good zinger later on when Bob had something over on her. The two kids could sense danger thick in the air and dared not utter a word.

After the ticket had been given officer Johnson sat down on the hot vinyl seat and snickered to himself. He's lucky I got a sense of humor, the officer thought. What a gooney bird. After a moment the giggle turned to a laugh and the thought occurred to him again: What a god-danged gooney bird. As the old sedan pulled away the officer's laugh went into a wheezing until tears appeared at the corners of the big man's eyes. "Gooney bird," the policeman gasped out-loud. "A god-dang gooney bird."

Bob drove away absolutely and completely unaware of the joy he was bringing to so many people.

The family putted along in tense silence until they had reached the second fast food joint. It too had a drive-through window. Not being a man who learned from experience, Bob followed the signs until he came to a stop just short of the plastic menu board. Father Bob, steaming metaphorically and physically, stared at his children. "Small cokes," he hissed out. "You're getting small cokes."

"Hello, welcome to Captain Chicken," the little speaker sputtered out on cue with no more emotion than if it had been a recording, "may I take your order?"

Bob steeled himself. "One large coke," he grit out between clinched teeth, "two small cokes, and one large coffee."

"I have an order for one large coke, two small cokes and one large coffee. Would you be liking any of our special crunchy-skin chicken today?"

Bob took a deep breath. "No," he rasped out, "absolutely not."

"OK. Your order comes to two eighty-three at the window."

Dad took a look around him, befuddled by success. He put the car in gear and crept around to the window. It was free of obstruction. He paused just before the window waiting for fate to bestow yet another punch line. When nothing happened he sided up to the window. A fat Anglo with a dark, pencil mustache, greasy hair and a skinny tie came to stick his hand out the window. "Two eighty-three," he said. Bob handed him the money. The man handed back change and the four beverages, just like that. Dad replayed the events over in his mind to convince himself that everything was copasetic. Nope, he thought, nothing went wrong that time.

The ease of the transaction took some of the edge off of dad, to say the least of what some liquid was doing for him.

The only thing annoying him at the moment was that he had to follow the expressway a good mile before he had another opportunity to turn around. But the coffee was good--even though it was too hot--and satisfying his thirst. To expedite the cooling, Bob removed the white plastic lid and blew into the steaming liquid.

The cap was splashed with the staining black beverage and some of it dribbled onto his forearm and trousers. He set the lid on the dash, upside-down, steering with the same hand holding the cup. He reached out with his other and asked his wife for a tissue.

Sharon had been day-dreaming about the protagonist in her afternoon movie. Strong, handsome and courageous, perhaps an antipode to her husband, the protagonist posited only silly, girlish, and romantic thoughts in mom's head. She lamented her husband's failings but had no serious thoughts of another. Maybe the key to understanding Sharon was the fact that she had no thoughts in particular. Though sweaty and sweltering, she was as calm and relaxed as could be. Her husband's stress never transferred itself; which was one of the reasons why he got so stressed. Bob always felt as if he had to blow the top of his head off before his wife would do anything. Sharon, the consummate and self-erasing blank slate, reacted to situations, but was rarely affected by them. "The tissues are in the back," Sharon said, thinking of the handkerchief the paramour had waved to the departing train. "Susan, hand your father a tissue."

Susan worked her upper body out of the cross strap of the safety belt and bent over to the box which was lying at her Brother's feet. Bobby, who was going out of his mind in the tense silence, seized the opportunity to antagonize and scooted his body down until he could put his foot over the opening.

"Quit," Susan said and gave his leg a slap.

Bobby pushed down even harder, holding his ground.

Bob was holding up his hand like a scrubbed surgeon watching the two streams of coffee dribble down his forearm. "Hurry up," he commanded. "It's dripping."

"Quit," Susan yelled and gave her brother a shove.

"Susan," mother instructed, "hurry up."

"Bobby's got his foot on it."

"Bobby, let your sister get a tissue for your father."

"Hurry up," snapped Bob, watching the dribble reach his elbow.

Susan finally succeeded in wrestling the box away from her brother and pulled a tissue out. Because she sensed the urgency in her father's voice, she wadded the tissue up and tossed it to the front seat. Bob, who was busy with the driving and the dribbles, watched the little ball of paper come over his shoulder and drop like a three-pointer square into the middle of the cup.

"Damn, damn," Bob yelled and frantically tried grab the wad, which was sinking fast.

As he jerked the wheel back and forth in conjunction with his little struggle he drifted just a little too far toward the curb. "Look out," shouted Sharon. The front left wheel just nipped the cement, but nipped it just hard enough to cause the front end to bounce. That bouncing traveled to the steering wheel which knocked the cup of steaming coffee out of Bob's hand. Directly below the hand was the crotch.

Bob's body went rigid as a board, his pelvis jutting toward the ceiling. The heat, intense at first, ramped quickly to unbearable. "YAAAAAAAAAAAA," he screeched trying to yank his pants off with the one hand that wasn't driving. "YA, YA, YA, YA, YA. Oh God. Oh God. YAAAAAAAAAAAAAA." In agony, he finally let go of the steering wheel and yanked his trousers to his knees with both hands. As he did so the car swerved sharply to the right and rammed the curb on the far side, blowing out the front right tire.

The other three in the car joined in with dad's screeching as the car rammed onto the curb and came to a rest. Other cars behind and to the side swerved, skidded, honked and cursed as the sedan went ballistic across the lane. After the thump, three of the four passengers went quiet. Bob continued his shrieking, body rigid, head pointed toward the ceiling, both hands trying to fend off the coffee soaked clothing.

"YAAAAAAAAA," the yells went on, finally starting to diminish in intensity. "Ya, ya, ooooooh god, god oh god."

People, who had been driven to a halt by the careening sedan got out of their car and, in a humanitarian gesture, came up to the damaged vehicle to assist. Sharon, now partially recovered from the impact, turned to her two children who were both starting to cry. "Children," she said calmly over dad's lingering howls, "you need to get out of the car and get onto the sidewalk. Let's go. Come on." People were close to the driver's window and advancing. Sharon kept her wits about her. Thinking quickly she reached into her purse and retrieved a feminine napkin. Pulling loose the adhesive strip she slapped it over her husband's privates.

Two young men, professional types with ties and suit jackets, leaned down to the driver's window. "Hey, are you OK?" one of them asked.

Sharon tried to act aloof. "Yes, we're fine," she said nonchalantly.

The two men looked at the half naked, groaning man, body still rigid as a board, the feminine napkin, and exchanged a glance of disbelief. "Uh, like what happened," the other one said.

"He spilt some hot coffee," Sharon said a-matter-of-factly.

The two men put the little puzzle together and winced at the thought. The first man whistled out an "ooooo-weee."

"You need some help?" the second asked.

"We'll manage."

Someone in the gathering crowd yelled something to the two men and the first relayed the message. "They said they called 911."

By the time the fire-truck, police and ambulance had arrived on the scene Bob had gone from groaning to a kind of breathless panting. Sharon had gotten some dry boxer shorts out of the luggage for her husband to cover himself. She thought that they would be the most comfortable thing to wear considering the circumstances and she was probably right. The way she helped him off with his soaked pants and helped him to slip on the undergarment reminded her of when she used to change Susan and Bobby. He even made the same sort of cute little gurgling noises. If she would have had some talc she would have splashed his little boiled-red backside. The boxers had bright pink stars on them and on one leg in black it read "Tiger" and on the other it read "Stud." Sharon hadn't noticed.

Susan and Bobby had been temporarily adopted by the clerk of the convenience store they had crashed in front of. Bobby was working on a sugar buzz from the complimentary purple slurpee and Susan had chosen a tootsie pop and was doing her best to develop a crush on the wide-eyed and tanned college boy. To Susan, at the moment, the crush was going to be the start of an eternal flame of love. By that evening she forgot his name.

Bob was sitting on the curb still panting like an over-heated dog. Paramedics were wondering exactly what to do with him. No-one was inclined to inspect the affected area and Bob was not inclined to allow them to. All they did was offer him a few cold packs to stuff in his shorts to make him a little bit more comfortable. When Bob, through a breathy, exhausted voice, finally convinced them he was going to be alright, they decided to pack up their equipment and return to the station.

One of the paramedics, lugging his big black suitcase of wares, walked past the attending officer, who had his back to him, and noticed him shaking. He was familiar with the officer and wanted to know why he was behaving so peculiar. Leaning around to see his face he could see tears streaming down the big face, convulsing in silent laughter.

"What the hell's wrong with you Johnson?" he asked.

Officer Johnson just shook his head and put his hands over his face.

One of the bystanders, a rough looking fellow in blue jeans and cowboy hat with a scruffy beard and tatoos, had volunteered to change the tire and was nearly done. He talked to Sharon as he did his work and was offering her all kinds of advice on how to drive. For some reason he could not get it straight in his mind that Bob and not Sharon had been driving. "Ya gots ta never get behind that wheel," he said, lower lip bulging with tobacco, "unless yer willing to do combat. That's the way to think of it. Combat." When he was done, Sharon offered him some money. The hairy gent offered up both hands, stood back and bugged out his eyes in an embellished bit of body language to refuse the cash. "Karma is my only reward," he said solemnly, then turned to start a slow amble down the road.

The crowd, by this time, had trickled down to only the family and convenience store clerk. The clerk led Bobby and Susan to their mother one on each hand. "Looks like you guys are getting ready to go," he said to Sharon.

"Thanks for your taking care of them," she said to the young man.

"His name's Hank," Susan filled in enthusiastically. "He goes to the State College here in town. He says we'll like Yosemite."

"Well, I got to get back to the store. Better luck from here on out." Then to the two children, "See ya."

Bobby started climbing into the car but Sharon stood and watched her flame depart. "Good-bye Hank," she called after him. When

Hank turned around to wave as he walked she yelled again, "Good-by Hank."

Sharon turned her attention to her wounded husband. He was still panting, though slower, and staring off into the sky, one hand supporting his seated position, the other holding the cold packs in position on his crotch. "Honey?" she said. "Are you ready to go?"

Bob licked his lips and took a couple of deep breaths. "I guess," he wheezed out.

Making a slow, determined attempt to stand, he wrapped one hand forward between his legs and the other from the back, keeping the pain-easing packages in place. Bow-legged as a cartoon cowboy he made an awkward shuffle to the passenger side. There was no argument about who should drive. Sharon opened the door for him. "Thanks," he mumbled to his wife, and slid into place. Sharon waited for a break in the cars whizzing past on the expressway before moving to the driver's side. She slammed the door. The key was still in the ignition.

Before turning on the car she reached over and stroked the side of her husband's face. "I guess we should just get you home and think about this tomorrow," she said.

Bob looked determined for a moment, and then slumped in abdication. "Yeah," he wheezed, "I guess it's all over for today. I'm beaten. Nothing else can go wrong. But let's not chance it."

"Oh honey," Sharon cooed, trying to make him feel better, "you aren't beaten. There was nothing to lose."

"I wanted to go today, damn it. I wanted to go so bad. Everything is ruined."

"We'll have six more days after this one. Now let's get you back to the house and into bed right under the swamp cooler. You'll feel better."

Sharon put the car into park and reached down to give the key a good twist. When the head came off in her hand, she brought it up for inspection. "What kind of key is this? Plastic?"